"Good night," Brad said outside her front door, and leaned forward to kiss Abby on the cheek.

Just to prove that they would be fine around each other at the wedding.

Except somehow his lips didn't meet her cheek.

Instead, they brushed against her lips. Very gently. Very lightly.

Rather than backing away sensibly, he found himself kissing her again. Then he drew back.

And her lips were parted very, very slightly. Inviting him. Telling him that it was the same for her—that right at this second, she wanted them to kiss, too.

Memories collided in his head. The first time he'd kissed her, in the moonlight among the roses. The first time he'd kissed her before making love. Kissing her over the anvil in Gretna Green, their first kiss as a married couple.

How he'd missed her.

How he wanted her.

And he couldn't help leaning forward again. This time, she let him deepen the kiss. And it felt as if every nerve end in his body had just burst into life after five years of bein

D1444138

Dear Reader,

I've always enjoyed reunion stories, and this one is especially dear to me as I've set it in my part of the world (a fictional town, but anyone who follows me on Facebook will know that beach!). I had to do some very tough research involving dog-friendly cafés, walking on the beach with the dog and actually trying doggy ice-cream myself (!)—and Archie thoroughly enjoyed being on my research team.

Everyone said Brad and Abby married too young, and when they divorced five years ago, it seemed that everyone was right... Until they were reunited at his sister's wedding. But will the hurdles that got in their way last time stop them from rekindling their romance the second time around? Can Brad convince Abby to give him a second chance?

I hope you enjoy their journey.

With love,

Kate Hardy

Reunited at
the Altar

—

Kate Hardy

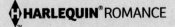
HARLEQUIN® ROMANCE

Recycling programs
for this product may
not exist in your area.

ISBN-13: 978-1-335-13520-9

Reunited at the Altar

First North American publication 2018

Copyright © 2018 by Pamela Brooks

Printed in U.S.A.

Kate Hardy has always loved books and could read before she went to school. She discovered Harlequin books when she was twelve and decided this was what she wanted to do. When she isn't writing, Kate enjoys reading, cinema, ballroom dancing and the gym. You can contact her via her website, katehardy.com.

Books by Kate Hardy

Harlequin Romance

Summer at Villa Rosa

The Runaway Bride and the Billionaire

Billionaires of London

Billionaire, Boss...Bridegroom?
Holiday with the Best Man

Falling for Mr. December
Falling for the Secret Millionaire
Her Festive Doorstep Baby
His Shy Cinderella
Christmas Bride for the Boss

Harlequin Medical Romance

Miracles at Muswell Hill Hospital

Christmas with Her Daredevil Doc
Their Pregnancy Gift

Paddington Children's Hospital

Mommy, Nurse...Duchess?

Unlocking the Italian Doc's Heart

Visit the Author Profile page
at Harlequin.com for more titles.

To Archie, my beloved spaniel, aka the newest member of my research team, who always keeps me company when I write.

Praise for
Kate Hardy

"I was hooked...*Her Festive Doorstep Baby* is a heart-tugging emotional romance."

—*Goodreads*

CHAPTER ONE

'ARE YOU SURE you're all right about this, Abby?' Ruby asked.

'Absolutely,' Abigail fibbed. 'I'm so pleased he agreed.'

That bit, at least, wasn't a lie. Abigail was more than pleased that Bradley Powell had not only agreed to come to his twin sister's wedding, he'd also promised to walk her down the aisle in their late father's stead—especially as he hadn't set foot in Great Crowmell, the Norfolk seaside town where they'd grown up, in the years since their father's funeral. Ruby had been panicking that Brad would make an excuse not to come to her wedding because he still couldn't face coming home.

As for actually seeing her ex-husband again for the first time since their divorce: that wasn't something Abigail relished. But she was five years older now. Infinitely wiser. She could do this. And she *would* do this with a smile, for Ruby's sake. No way was she going to rain on her best friend's parade.

'You know you can bring a date to the wedding,' Ruby said. 'Just give me a name for when it comes to sorting out the place cards. Or you don't even have to do that— bring whoever you like and I'll get someone to write his name on the place card that morning.'

'Thanks, but I don't need a date. I'm going to be way too busy on the day for that,' Abigail said with a smile. 'I've got chief bridesmaid duties to think about, and I want everything to go perfectly for your wedding.' The fact she'd barely dated since her divorce was irrelevant.

Or—a nasty thought hit her—was Ruby trying to tell her something? That she should bring a date, because Brad was bringing his new love to meet everyone and it would be awkward if Abigail turned up alone?

'Is Brad bringing a date?' Abigail asked, trying her best to sound casual and hoping that her suddenly thumping heart didn't show in her voice.

'Of course he's not. He's married to his j…' Ruby winced and clapped a hand to her mouth. 'Um.'

Abigail smiled and finished the phrase. 'Married to his job.' *Whereas he'd once been married to me.* And she knew that was exactly what Ruby was thinking, too.

'Sorry, Abby. I didn't mean to—'

Abigail hugged her best friend. 'It's fine. That water's so far under the bridge, it's already been recycled twice. Brad and I can be civil to each other.' She hoped. She'd been through all the stages of grief at the end of their marriage. Denial that it was over, anger that he was being so stubborn, bargaining with him to see sense, depression when she realised that she just wasn't enough for him, and finally acceptance that it was all over. All laced together with guilt, because she'd been the one to instigate the end.

She'd been so sure that if she walked out on him and went home to her parents, it would shock him into his senses: that he'd miss her and realise that shutting her out wasn't the answer.

And how wrong she'd been. Because, instead of asking her to come back to him, Brad had simply said that her defection was proof that everyone had been right about them. They'd been way too young to get married, they weren't going to make it, and he'd give her a divorce so she could have the chance to make a real life for herself.

Divorce had been the last thing she'd wanted.

But Brad had built a wall of ice around himself after his father's death. He'd shut Abigail out, and she just hadn't been able to reach him. Despite being married for nearly four years, they hadn't been strong enough to weather the storm. She hadn't supported him enough in his grief or been able to hold her marriage together.

So maybe everyone had been right about their relationship, after all. They'd been naive and reckless and immature, eloping to Gretna Green the week before their exam results. Everyone else had thought they were simply doing the coast-to-coast walk from St Bees in the Lake District to Robin Hood's Bay in Yorkshire, raising money for the local lifeboat rescue team—which they had. They'd just happened to go to St Bees via Gretna Green, having quietly sorted out all the marriage paperwork the day after their last exams.

At the time, they'd both thought that eloping would be romantic. That each other was The One. That their love would last for ever.

Yeah. Naive, reckless and immature just about summed it up.

And she wasn't any of those any more.

'Is Brad OK with me being your bridesmaid?' Abigail asked. 'If he's not, you know I'll step down and keep out of the way on the actual day—but obviously I'll still help you with all the organisation and do anything you need.'

Ruby rolled her eyes. 'For goodness' sake. Who else was I going to ask to be my chief bridesmaid, other than the person who's been my best friend since the day we met at toddler group?'

And who also happened to be her twin's ex-wife.

'Have you actually told him?' Abigail asked.

'Yes. And he—well, he said the same that you did. That you could be perfectly civil to each other at the wedding.'

Civil. All that passion and love and hope reduced to cool, dismissive politeness. It made Abigail want to weep. What a waste.

Not that she was going to let Ruby have the slightest idea about that. Abigail wanted her best friend's wedding day to be the happiest day of her life and she'd do her best to make it happen. 'There you go, then. All's fine.' Abigail smiled. 'Now, we have lists to make. If you will insist on having a whirl-wind wedding…'

Ruby snorted. 'Says the woman who eloped.'

'There's a lot to be said for keeping it simple,' Abigail said lightly. 'No worries about seating plans, menus or dresses.'

Ruby looked at her. 'Do you regret it, Abby?'

'Marrying your brother? Or eloping?' Abigail asked.

'You know what I'm asking.'

Abigail sighed. 'I don't regret marrying Brad. I loved him. We just brought the wedding forward to before he went away to study rather than waiting until after he'd finished his degree, that was all.' It had been Brad's idea to elope and, although part of Abby had thought it wasn't really practical to get married when he was about to go away and be a student, she'd been madly in love with him and thought he felt the same about her. So she'd said yes, squashing her misgivings.

'But you regret eloping?'

'Yes and no. Yes, it was romantic and fun to elope.' Just the two of them. And they'd made love so tenderly in their cheap hotel room that night. Eighteen years old, with the whole world ahead of them. 'But, in hindsight,' Abigail said, 'I regret not sharing the day with everyone else. It meant Dad didn't get to walk me down the aisle, our mums didn't get the chance to dress up and make a fuss, you weren't my bridesmaid, and your dad wasn't the best man. Looking back, I realise we were selfish. We should've shared that day.' And maybe if they'd been mature enough to share their wedding, they would've been mature enough to make their marriage last.

'Anyway, there's no point in dwelling on it because you can't change the past.' Abigail opened up her laptop. 'Right. Our list of things to do starts here...'

Six weeks later

Great Crowmell.

Even the signpost made Brad's stomach turn to knots.

The town where he'd grown up.

The town where he'd met the love of his life.

The town where he'd lost her.

He was dreading this. He'd avoided coming here at all since his father's funeral—not for birthdays, not for Christmases, not for an off-the-cuff visit. The longer he left it, the

harder it was to face. He'd seen his family—
of *course* he had—but not here. He'd met
them in London, organised posh afternoon
teas and trips to the theatre with hard-to-get
tickets, to make up for not coming here.

Every nerve in his body told him to turn
the car round again and drive back to London. Back to where he could bury himself in
work and forget everything.

But he couldn't be that selfish. His sister
was getting married and he had no intention
of letting her down. This was the one thing
that would make him come back: Ruby had
asked him to walk her down the aisle on her
wedding day and he'd promised her he'd do
it. Even though the last time he'd set foot in
that church and walked down that aisle, he'd
been one of the pallbearers carrying their
father's coffin, he'd suck up his feelings for
her sake.

Though Brad hadn't quite been able to face
going back to stay in their childhood home,
filled with his memories of their father—and
with a hefty loading of guilt. Instead, he'd
rented a holiday cottage for a few days. One
of the ancient two-up, two-down fishermen's
cottages in the flint-built terraces just behind
the harbour. A place with no memories, so he
had a bolthole when the town and everything

that went with it got too much for him: all the kindness and concern edged with speculation and gossip. He knew that Ruby understood and he hoped she'd talk their mother round. He wasn't avoiding Rosie; he was avoiding the house. Just as he'd done for the last five years. He knew it was selfish, and it made the guilt worse.

And then there was Abigail.

How was he going to face her?

More layers of guilt weighed down on him. He'd been the one to sweep her off her feet and ask her to elope with him; and when life threw its first hurdle in their way he'd let her down. He'd let her go.

Even before Ruby had diffidently asked if he'd mind that Abigail would be her chief bridesmaid, Brad had known who she'd choose—the woman who'd been her best friend right from toddler group through to high school and beyond. He'd prepared himself for it so when it came, he was able to tell Ruby without batting an eyelid that everything was absolutely fine, and he and Abigail could be perfectly civil to each other on the day. But stupidly he hadn't thought to ask Ruby if Abigail was taking anyone to the wedding. The idea of seeing his ex-wife dancing with her new man, laughing and smiling and kissing him in the moonlight, the way she'd once done with him, made him feel sick.

He dragged in a breath. Maybe he should've asked one of his colleagues to be his plus one, just in case. There was still time; the wedding wasn't until Saturday. Though who could he ask, without either giving out the wrong signals—and he really didn't want the complication of someone at work thinking he was interested in a relationship—or having to explain the situation and becoming an object of pity throughout the lab and the office?

Maybe he should've made an excuse not to come to the wedding in the first place. Maybe he should've said he was speaking at a conference and, because Ruby had only given him a few weeks' notice, there simply wasn't enough time to find someone to take his place.

But then he'd hate himself for letting her down.

He needed to brace himself and deal with it. Be the cool, calm, analytical scientist he'd spent the last five years turning himself into. The one who kept his feelings completely locked away and could deal with almost anything without betraying a flicker of emotion. There was no place in his professional life for guilt, for nervousness and wondering how people were going to react to him, so he shouldn't let any of that have a place in his personal life, either.

He could do this. The taste of bile in his mouth, the way his hands felt cold and tingling with adrenaline—that was all psychosomatic and he was going to ignore it. And he'd grab some paracetamol to deal with the tension headache that had started more than an hour ago, as soon as he'd crossed the county border to Norfolk.

He pulled into the car park in the middle of the town, fed coins into the meter to get a pay-and-display car park ticket to tide him over to the next morning, and stuck the ticket on the inside of his windscreen.

The letting agent had warned him that parking was tricky outside the rented cottage so he left the car and made his way to the address. He pulled up the four-digit key code for the safe box where the house keys were stored from the last email from the letting agent on his phone, retrieved the keys and dumped his luggage next to the stairs in the living room. When he headed into the kitchen at the back, there was a tray on the small kitchen table containing a plate, a mug, a spoon, a box of tea-bags and a tin of good instant coffee. There was also a white paper bag, and a note propped on top of it.

Welcome to 2 Quay Cottages. There's milk and butter in the fridge, bread in the cupboard, and a little something in the paper bag to keep you going until dinner. Any problems, please call in at number 1.

Clearly the neighbour was happy to act as a kind of caretaker. That was reassuring, given that the letting agent was in London. OK, Brad thought, and opened the paper bag.

A blueberry muffin.

Home-made? he wondered. From the neighbour? Though surely the neighbour would've put his or her name on the note. Or maybe they'd been interrupted while they were writing the note and simply forgot to sign it. Whatever, the gesture was appreciated.

Brad realised then that he was hungry. He'd worked through his lunch break so he could leave early and miss the worst of the rush-hour traffic for his three-hour drive from London to north Norfolk, but then he'd been too keyed up to eat when he'd stopped for a rest break. He hadn't bothered to stop at the

large supermarket on the edge of town—one
that hadn't been there on his last visit—and
he hadn't even thought about dinner. He'd just
been focused on driving to Great Crowmell
and facing all the memories.

He took a bite of the muffin. And it was
fabulous.

For a second, he was transported back to
the early days of his marriage. When Abby
had made blueberry muffins for breakfast
on Sunday mornings, and he'd woken to the
smell of good coffee and cake. They'd always
eaten the muffins in bed and lazed around
until lunchtime...

He shook himself. Long, long gone.

Coffee. That would sort out his head. And
it would help the paracetamol to tackle his
headache, too.

He took the kettle to the sink and turned
on the tap.

Nothing.

The neighbour hadn't left a note about there
being any problems with the water.

Frowning, he went upstairs to the bathroom
and tried the taps on the sink and the bath.
Nothing there, either. When he flushed the
toilet, the cistern didn't fill up. Clearly someone had turned off the stopcock, for some rea-

son, and forgotten to turn it back on. It would be easy enough to fix.

But he couldn't actually find the stopcock. The obvious place for it to be located was under the sink in the kitchen, but it wasn't there—or in any of the other cupboards. It wasn't in the bathroom, either.

Great.

It looked as if he was going to have to disturb the occupant of number one, after all, to see if he or she knew what the water problem was and where the stopcock was located.

Leaving the little cottage, he walked to the neighbouring house and knocked on the white-painted front door. And he stared in utter shock when it opened, putting him face to face with Abigail Scott for the first time in nearly five years.

CHAPTER TWO

'BRAD?' ABIGAIL LOOKED as shocked as he felt, the colour draining from her face as she stared at him. 'What are you doing here?' she asked—at exactly the same time as he asked, 'What are you doing here?'

'I was looking for the owner of number one Quay Cottages,' he said.

'That would be me.' She frowned. 'So that means you're hiring number two this week?'

'Didn't the letting agency tell you?'

'They don't always give me a name. They just said it was a single person who'd booked a Monday-to-Monday let.'

Which was clearly why she'd left him the fresh muffin today as a welcome gift. 'I didn't realise you lived here.'

'No.' She raised an eyebrow, as if to point out that it was really none of his business, since he was no longer married to her. 'I assume there's a problem next door?'

'Yes. There's no water,' he said.

'Ah.' She grimaced. 'Number three had a leaking pipe and the plumber borrowed the spare keys from me to turn off your water this morning, just in case it caused a problem in your house. Obviously he forgot to turn the water back on before he returned the keys, and I didn't check because I assumed he would've already done that.'

'And the stopcock isn't in an obvious place.'

'When these cottages were done up, let's just say the building contractors made some unusual choices,' she said. 'I'll come and show you where it is.'

'Thanks.'

Abigail looked hardly any different from the way she'd looked five years ago, when Brad had last seen her. She was still the most beautiful woman he'd ever met, with eyes that he remembered being sea-green when she was happy and grey when she was sad, a heart-shaped face and a perfect cupid's bow mouth. The striking difference was the way she wore her dark hair; he remembered it falling halfway down her back, and now it was cropped in a short pixie cut that made her grey-green eyes look huge.

'Audrey Hepburn,' he said.

She frowned. 'What?'

'Your hair. *Breakfast at Tiffany's*.'

She inclined her head. 'Thank you, but actually she had long hair for that film. This is more like her hair was in *Sabrina*.'

Of course Abigail would know. She and Ruby loved Hepburn's films and had binge-watched them as teens in the summer holidays. And it was a stupid thing to say. 'Sorry.'

'It's not important.' She ushered him out of the house, and waited for him to let her into the cottage next door. 'OK. The stopcock's here in the lean-to at the back.'

He found the right key, unlocked the door and dealt with the stopcock.

'I'll wait to make sure the water's working,' she said. 'And I'd better ask the agency to put a note about the stopcock's position in the file they leave for clients.'

'Good idea,' he said. Abigail always had been practical and organised. She'd made him feel grounded and back in the real world after a hard day at the lab—and he'd missed that.

Not that he had a right to miss it.

He'd been the one to insist on a divorce. Even though he'd been sure he was doing the right thing for her, he knew it had hurt her.

There was nothing he could do to change the past; but he wanted things to be at least on an even keel between them, for the sake of Ruby's wedding.

'Thank you for helping,' he said, turning on the taps and noting that thankfully the water ran clear.

'No problem.'

Abigail knew this was her cue to leave, and to make herself a little bit scarce over the next few days.

Except Brad looked like hell, with dark smudges under his eyes. And she knew why: because he was back in Great Crowmell for the first time since his father's death. Home, where he felt he'd failed. Even though Jim's death most definitely hadn't been his fault, Brad had blamed himself, and that was when their life together had started to unravel.

They were divorced, she reminded herself. This was none of her business.

But Bradley Powell had been her first love. Her one and only love, if she was honest with herself. Right now, she could see he was suffering. She couldn't just leave him like this. OK, so she knew he didn't love her any more and she'd learned to accept that; but, for the sake of what he'd once been to her, she wanted to help him.

'Are you OK?' she asked, her voice gentle.

'Yes.'

He was lying. Putting a wall between them, the same way he'd done five years ago. She could walk away, like she had last time; or, this time, she could challenge him. Push him the way she maybe should've pushed him back then, except at the age of twenty-two she hadn't quite had the confidence to do that.

Now, things were different. She knew who she was and she was comfortable in her own skin. And she was no longer afraid to challenge him. 'That's the biggest load of rubbish I've heard in a while.'

He looked at her as if not quite believing what he'd heard. 'What?'

'You're not OK, Brad,' she said. 'You're lying about it—which is crazy, because I'm the last person you should need to keep a stiff upper lip in front of—and I'm calling you on it.'

He lifted his chin, as if to argue. 'I...' Then the fight went out of him and he sighed. 'No. You're right. I'm not OK.'

'Because you're dreading this week?' she asked. 'That's why you booked into the cottage, isn't it? So you wouldn't have to go home and see the ghosts.'

He raked a hand through his hair. 'You always could see through me, Abby. Except back then...'

'Back then, I would've let you get away with it.' How young and naive she'd been. In the last five years she'd grown much wiser. Stronger, more able to deal with tricky situations. She'd changed. But had Brad? 'You've just had a three-hour drive from London, in rush-hour traffic. I'm guessing you didn't have time for lunch and you were thinking about your current project while you were driving, so you didn't bother to get any shopping on the way here either. Apart from what I left you, your fridge and cupboards are all empty. But there's an easy solution. Come and sit in my kitchen while I make you something to eat.'

He shook his head. 'I can't ask you to do that.'

She folded her arms and looked at him. 'You're not asking me. I'm telling you.'

'Bossy.' But there was the hint of a smile in the tiny crinkles at the corners of his eyes. A smile she wished she hadn't noticed, because it still had the power to make her knees weak.

We're divorced, she reminded herself. I'm just doing this for Ruby, to make sure Brad doesn't get overwhelmed by the past and bail out on her before the wedding. Bradley Powell doesn't make my knees go weak any more. He *doesn't*.

'Just shut up and come next door,' she said, more to cover her own confusion than anything else.

'Is there anything I can do to help?' Brad asked when he'd followed her into her kitchen.

Abigail shook her head and gestured to the small bistro table in the nook that served as a dining area. 'Sit down and make yourself comfortable.'

'Thank you.' He paused. 'So how long have you been living here?'

'Two years. Didn't Ruby tell you?'

'She doesn't really talk to me about you.' He looked at her. 'Does she talk to you about me?'

'No,' she said. 'Though obviously your mum told me you'd got your doctorate. She showed me the graduation photos.'

He'd nearly not bothered with the graduation ceremony—until his sister had pointed out that she and their mother would quite like to be there, so it would be a bit selfish of him not to go. Brad had felt he didn't deserve the fuss, but he'd given in for his mother's sake.

'Uh-huh.' He didn't want to talk to Abigail about his graduation and how much he'd missed his father. How it had been a physical ache. How he'd longed to say to Jim, 'See, I told you I'd make something of myself doing the subject I love.'

He grabbed at the nearest excuse to change the subject. 'Nice house.' It looked as if it was the same layout as the cottage he'd hired for the week: the white-painted front door opened straight into the living room, and stairs led between the living room and kitchen to the upper floor. But whereas next door was all furnished in neutral shades, as far as he'd seen, Abigail had gone for bright colour. Her living room was painted a warm primrose yellow, with deep red curtains and a matching deep red sofa opposite the cast-iron original fireplace with a huge mirror above it, a wall full of books and a massive stylised painting of a peacock on another wall, which looked very much like his sister's handiwork. And the kitchen walls here were painted a light, bright teal; the cupboards were cream and the worktop was grey. It was stylish and homely at the same time.

The perfect size for two.

He didn't let himself think about who might have sat at this table opposite her. It was none of his business who she dated. She wasn't his wife any more.

'Are there any dietary things I need to know about?' she asked.

'Such as?'

She shrugged. 'I know you don't have any food allergies, but you might have given up eating meat or fish since we last ate together.'

Had she? He really had no idea. As for himself, he barely noticed what he ate, since she'd left. Since he'd pushed her into leaving, he amended mentally. 'No. Nothing's changed. But I don't want to put you to any trouble. I can walk up the road and get some fish and chips—assuming the chip shop's still there on the harbour, that is?'

'You're not putting me to any trouble,' she said. 'I haven't eaten yet this evening. It's as quick to cook for two as it is for one.'

'Then, if you're sure you don't mind, whatever you want to cook is absolutely fine with me,' he said. 'Thank you.'

'You told Ruby we could be civil. So did I. We might as well start here and now.'

'A truce. OK.' He could do that. And maybe, if he could get things on an even keel with her, it would take some of the weight of guilt from him.

'Coffee?'

'Thanks. I'd love one.' He paused. 'That

muffin you left next door—did you make that
yourself?'

'Yes. This morning.'

'I appreciated it. And it was very good.'

'Thank you.'

She'd gone slightly pink. Was she remembering when she'd made muffins in his
student days and they'd eaten them in bed together? Not that he could ask her. That was
way, way too intimate.

She made coffee just the way he liked it,
strong and sugarless with a just dash of milk.
He remembered how she took her coffee, too.
And the fact that she never drank tea. Funny
how all the memories flooded back, as if their
years apart had never happened.

Wishful thinking. It was way too late to do
anything about it now.

She chopped onions, chilli and garlic, then
heated oil in a pan and started to sauté them.
The kitchen smelled amazing. She added
diced chicken, and he realised just how hungry he was. Abigail always had been good in
the kitchen; rather than going away to study
for a degree, she'd planned to join her family's café business when she left school. She
was going to work her way up while he studied, and they were going to get married after
he graduated.

Until Brad, after a huge row with his dad, had rebelled; he'd asked Abby to elope with him before they got their exam results. All wide-eyed and trusting, young and full of hope, she'd agreed. And she'd put her plans aside, moving with him when he left for university, getting a job in a café in Cambridge and ending up managing the place within a year.

Ruby had been economical with the details but Brad guessed that, after Abigail had moved back to Great Crowmell, she'd gone with her original Plan A and joined the family business. Given that her parents were in their late fifties and would be looking at retiring, he'd guess that she was taking more responsibility every year. Maybe she was even running the place now.

'So how's the café?' he asked.

'Fine. How's the lab?'

'Fine.'

Stonewalling each other with single-word answers wasn't going to do anything to help the situation. Brad decided to make the effort and try some polite conversation. Offer some information, which might make her offer information in return. 'My team's working on developing a new antibiotic.'

'Sounds good—we definitely need that.' She paused. 'So are you happy in London?'

He hadn't been happy in the last five years. But he did like his job. And she was asking about his job, right? 'Yes. How about you? You're happy here at the café?' If he focused on work rather than the personal stuff, then she wouldn't tell him about her new love.

'Yes, I'm happy at the café. Like you, I'm developing something, except mine's rather more frivolous.' She paused, then said brightly, 'Ice cream for dogs.'

'Ice cream for dogs?' The idea was so incongruous that it made him smile.

'Don't knock it,' she said, smiling back. 'Think how many people bring their dogs to the beach, then come and sit with them outside the café.'

He knew that Scott's Café, on the edge of the beach, had tables outside as well as inside, plus water bowls for dogs; it had always been dog-friendly, even before it became trendy to welcome dogs.

'Half of the customers buy an ice cream for their dogs to help cool them down, too, but obviously the sugar's not good for the dogs' teeth and the fat's not brilliant for their diet, either,' Abby said. 'So we've produced something a bit more canine-friendly.'

He raised an eyebrow. 'So you're telling me you're making chicken-flavoured ice cream?'

She laughed. 'Not quite. It's more like frozen yoghurt. We do a carrot and cinnamon one, and a cheese one.'

He stared at her. 'Cheese ice cream?'

'They serve Parmesan ice cream at the posh restaurant round the bay in Little Crowmell,' she said. 'That's what gave me the idea. Especially as Waffle—' her parents' dachshund '—will do anything for cheese. He loved being one of my beta testers. So did your mum's dog.'

He wondered who'd taken her to Little Crowmell and had to damp down an unexpected flicker of jealousy. He had no right to be jealous. She was a free agent. It was up to her who she dated, he reminded himself yet again.

'Dinner smells nice,' he said, reverting to a safer subject.

'It's not that fancy. Just chicken arrabbiata.'

He'd always loved her cooking. 'It's still better than I could've made.' Not that he really cooked, any more. Cooking for one didn't seem worth the effort, when he was tired after a long day in the lab. It was so much easier to buy something from the chiller cabinet in the supermarket and shove it in the microwave for a couple of minutes. Something he didn't have to think about or even taste.

Abigail's chicken arrabbiata tasted even better than it smelled.

And how weird it was to be eating with her again, in this intimate little galley kitchen, at this tiny little table. Close enough so that, when he moved his feet, he ended up touching hers.

'Sorry,' he said, moving his feet swiftly away again and banging his ankle on the chair leg.

She gave him a half-shrug. 'Not a problem.'

She might be immune to him nowadays, he thought, but he was far from immune to her. There was a time when they would've sat at a tiny table like this together, their bare feet entwined. When they would've shared glances. When dinner would've been left half-eaten because he would've scooped her up and carried her up the stairs to their bed.

And he really wasn't going to let himself wonder if she slept in a double bed.

It was none of his business.

This was supposed to be civil politeness. A truce. Getting rid of the awkwardness between them, so Ruby's wedding would go smoothly at the weekend. So why did he feel so completely off balance?

He forced himself to finish the pasta—she was right, he did need to eat—and then cleared the table for her while she rummaged in the freezer.

She was close enough to touch.

And that way danger lay. Physical contact between them would be a very, very bad idea. Because seeing her again had brought back way too many memories—along with a huge sense of loneliness and loss.

He retreated to the bistro table, and she brought over two bowls, spoons and a plastic tub.

'Are you selling tubs for people to take home, nowadays?' he asked, suddenly curious.

'Yes, but they're half-litre paper cartons rather than like this. Ruby designed them for me—pink and white Regency stripes, with "Scott's" written across it in black script,' Abigail said.

'So you're expanding the business?'

She inclined her head. 'Certain local restaurants stock our ice cream, and we have pop-up ice cream stalls for events. Regency-style carts. Ruby's having one at her wedding.'

And how different his sister's wedding would be from his own. A big affair, with the church filled with family and friends. The complete opposite from his and Abby's: no frills, no fuss, just the two of them, and two witnesses that the wedding planner at Gretna Green had provided. Abby had worn an ordinary but pretty summer dress and carried a posy of cream roses, and he'd worn the suit his mother had bought him for his interview at Cambridge. It had got a bit creased in his rucksack, but he hadn't cared. He'd just wanted to get married to Abby and be with her for ever and ever, and prove to his dad that he was wrong, that they weren't too young and he wouldn't find someone else in the first week away at university—that their marriage would last.

The summer when they were eighteen.

How young and foolish they'd both been.

All that was left from that day now was a handful of photographs.

He shook himself. They were meant to be talking about her business, not their past. 'Sounds good,' he said lightly. 'So what's this?'

'A new flavour. I'm still tweaking it, so it's not in production yet. Let me know what you think.'

She actually wanted his opinion? Something shifted inside him.

She put a scoop into the bowl. 'If you hate it, don't be polite and eat it—just tell me what you don't like about it because that'll be much more useful. I also have salted caramel in the freezer.'

His favourite. And he knew that she remembered. Just as he remembered that she loathed chocolate ice cream.

He looked at the bowl she'd just given him. The ice cream was a dusky pink, studded with pieces of deep red fruit. He took a spoonful. 'No more tweaks needed,' he said. 'Cherry and almond.'

'Cherry and amaretto, actually—but that's close enough.' She looked pleased. 'So the amaretto isn't overpowering?'

He tried another spoonful. 'No. You've got a good balance. It's not too sour from the cherries, but it's also not oversweet.'

'Analysed like a true scientist.'

There was amusement in her voice, but there was also respect. And maybe, he thought, a note of affection? But he'd managed to kill her love for him, five years ago. He'd shut her out, hadn't let her help him deal with the shock of his father's death. He didn't deserve her affection. 'It saves time,' he said.

'Thanks. I thought I might have got it right

with this batch, though I was thinking about adding pieces of crushed amaretti biscuits.'

He shook his head. 'It'll change the texture too much. This is rich and soft and—well, *nice.*'

'Good. Help yourself to more. Or there's salted caramel,' she said.

He realised then that he'd finished the bowl. 'I'm fine,' he said. 'But thank you.'

He insisted on doing the washing up. And, even though he knew he really ought to go, how could he refuse when she offered him another coffee?

Her living room was just as cosy as the kitchen.

'Is that one of Ruby's?' he asked, gesturing towards the peacock.

'Yes. It was a special commission,' she said with a smile. Then she grew serious. 'It's going to be hard for you, this week.'

There was no point in lying. He knew she'd see through it. 'Yes.'

'I imagine you came back early so you could face things before the wedding on Saturday, instead of being hit by the whole lot on the day.'

How well she knew him. 'It seemed the most sensible approach.' Doing the lot in one day tomorrow would be easiest in the long run; and if he did it now he'd cope better at the wedding.

'I'm working tomorrow,' she said, 'but I'm pretty much off duty from Wednesday so I can help Ruby with any last-minute details.' She paused. 'If you want someone to go with you to…' She paused, and he knew what she wasn't saying. To the church. To his father's grave. To all the places in the town that held so many memories, they threatened to choke him. 'Well, you know where I am,' she finished.

It was a really generous offer, especially considering how he'd pushed her away before.

But he also knew he had to face this on his own. 'Thanks, but I'm fine.'

Brad wasn't fine. Abigail could see it in his dark, dark eyes.

But he was as stubborn as his father had been. Which wasn't always a good thing. He was making himself miserable, and that made his family miserable. Why couldn't he see that?

'Brad. It's been five years.' And everyone else had moved on, except Brad himself. 'I hope by now you've worked out that you weren't to blame.'

He said nothing.

'Your dad was a stubborn old coot. I loved Jim dearly, but he didn't help himself and he didn't listen to anyone.' Maybe now wasn't the right time to say it—but then again, when would be the right time? 'I think you're going the same way.'

'What?'

There was a simmering, dangerous tone to his voice. But Abigail wasn't backing down now. It was a boil that had needed lancing years ago. The poison needed to come out so Brad could move on instead of being stuck in the misery of the past. 'Jim was the one to blame for his death, not you. If he'd listened to his doctor and taken his angina medication out with him on the boat—or, better still, waited until the following weekend when you could've gone out on the boat with him and he wouldn't have been on his own—he wouldn't have had the heart attack in the first place; or at least if he'd had his GTN spray with him he would've been able to buy himself enough time for the emergency services to get to him and treat him in time.'

He clenched his jaw. 'My dad's *dead*.'

'And you're still alive, Brad.' Though he wasn't living. Just existing. 'Stop wearing that hair shirt and thinking you have to atone for something that really wasn't your fault.'

His face shuttered. 'I don't want to have this conversation.'

'No,' she said, not sure whether she was more angry or sad. 'You wouldn't face it then and you won't face it now. Brad, for pity's sake—you might want to keep punishing yourself, and that's your choice, but please make sure you don't punish your mum and Ruby at the same time.'

'I think,' he said, 'I'd better go. Before we say something we'd both regret.'

He was shutting her out again and refusing to discuss anything. So he hadn't changed. How stupid she was to think that five years might have made a difference. 'You do that,' she said. 'But if you're not smiling all day until your face hurts on Saturday, then you'll answer to me.'

His eyes widened as if he was shocked that she could even think that he'd do anything less than be delighted for his twin. 'Ruby's my sister.'

'And you've been there for her?' It was a rhetorical question, because they both knew the answer. He hadn't. He'd shut himself away in his lab, suffering in silence and not letting anyone comfort him—and that had also meant he wasn't able to comfort anyone else.

A muscle worked in his jaw. 'That's none of your business.'

'That's the attitude you took when it *was* still my business,' she said. 'Stubborn, refusing to see any other point of view except your own.' The anger she hadn't realised she was suppressing flared up, and the words came out before she could stop them. 'That's what killed your dad. Don't let it kill you, too.'

He stood up, his dark eyes full of answering anger, and walked out without a word.

He didn't even slam the door behind him. Just left it open.

Abigail stared after him, the flash of anger suddenly gone and leaving her full of guilt.

Oh, God. What had she done?

She was supposed to be civil to the man and start pouring oil at the first sign of any troubled waters. But instead she'd stirred up the storm. Big time.

OK.

Tomorrow, she'd apologise. And hope that she could repair the damage in time for Ruby's wedding.

CHAPTER THREE

EVEN THOUGH BRAD was tired after the three-hour drive, he couldn't sleep. He just stared into the darkness, replaying Abby's words over and over again in his head.

'You might want to keep punishing your-self, and that's your choice, but please make sure you don't punish your mum and Ruby.'

Was he punishing his mother and his twin?

'Stubborn, refusing to see any other point of view except your own. That's what killed your dad.'

No, what had killed his dad was Brad's selfishness.

He should've come home for the weekend and gone out on the boat with his dad, instead of going off with Abby for a romantic weekend away. OK, so she'd won the trip in a competition, but she could've taken Ruby with her instead and made it a girly weekend: and then Brad would've been there for Jim.

He would've made sure that his dad had his angina medication with him on the boat. He could've administered it, bought time until the emergency services could get to them.

Though he was horribly aware that Abby had said pretty much the same thing. If only Jim had listened to his doctor and taken his medication with him. If only Jim had waited.

But everyone knew that James Powell was a Type A personality and the word 'wait' simply wasn't in his vocabulary. Jim was a larger-than-life character, a sharp barrister who'd lived for his job and been bored stiff being stuck at home. Of course he wouldn't have waited to go out on the boat until someone else could be with him. He would've argued that he was perfectly capable of crewing the boat alone. He'd hated the whole idea of having to retire early on the grounds of poor health. Being diagnosed with a heart condition that could kill him if it wasn't kept under control had been the worst thing that could've happened to him. He'd needed something to fill his time, and the boat was the one thing that had stopped him going crazy.

If Brad had only come home, that weekend...

But he hadn't.

And Jim had taken the boat out on his own.

He'd had an angina attack and collapsed. The chest pain had been so bad, he hadn't even been able to call the emergency services; he'd only been capable of hitting the last number redial on his phone.

Brad's number.

'Chest. Hurts. On boat. Call coastguard,' he'd gasped.

'I'll do it now. Where's your medication, Dad?' Brad asked.

'Home.'

Meaning that there had been nothing to help with the pain.

Abby had been in the spa, having a facial, but thankfully she'd left her mobile phone in their room. With shaking hands, Brad had put his dad on speaker on his own phone and called the emergency services from Abby's.

'I'm getting someone to you now, Dad.'

'Should've waited.' Jim had squeezed the pain-filled words out.

'That doesn't matter now, Dad. Stay with me. Stay with me. It's going to be OK. I've got help coming. I know it hurts to talk, so I just want one word from you every couple of minutes so I know you're still with me. OK?'

'Yes.'

'Stay with me, Dad. I love you. It's going to be all right.'

But Jim had been in trouble way before the helicopter and the lifeboat had reached him. Miles and miles away from the coast, knowing it would take him hours to drive to Great Crowmell even if he left the hotel that very second, Brad had been unable to do anything to help. He'd heard the clatter of the phone onto the deck and guessed that his dad had dropped it.

'Dad! Dad! Stay with me. Pick up the phone. Please pick up the phone,' he'd pleaded.

But Jim hadn't answered. All Brad had been able to hear was the hum of the engine and the screaming of the seagulls, until finally the phone had been picked up by one of the lifeboat crew.

'This is the lifeboat. We've winched down the paramedic from the helicopter. You're his son, who called us out, right?'

'Yes.'

'OK. We're going to fly your dad back to hospital. Can you give us some information?'

'Anything you need,' Brad had said, and had gone through his father's medical history.

But it had been too late.

Jim had had a massive heart attack in the helicopter and the crew hadn't been able to resuscitate him. He'd died on the way to hospital.

Stop wearing that hair shirt and thinking you have to atone for something that really wasn't your fault.

Now that was where Abby was wrong. Brad didn't blame himself for his father's death. Even if he'd been there, if he'd given his father the medication, there was a very high chance that Jim would still have had that heart attack and died on the way to hospital.

That wasn't what crucified him every single day.

It was the fact that he'd been the last person to speak to Jim while he was still alive—while his father was still conscious—and he'd known that he couldn't do a thing to save his dad. That the lifeboat and the air ambulance wouldn't get to him in time. And then, in the days after the funeral, he'd realised that he would never get the chance to prove to his dad that he'd made the right career choice, following his heart to become a scientist rather than following in Jim's footsteps and becoming a barrister.

Brad just hadn't been able to cope with it all. To keep himself functioning, he'd had to build a wall round his heart. And that hadn't been fair to Abby: so he'd done the right thing by the love of his life. He'd set her free to find happiness with someone else.

And she thought he was being self-indulgent and wearing a hair shirt?

He stared into the darkness.

If only things had been different.

If only.

Eventually, he slept. His dreams were vivid, to the point where he actually reached out for her, the next morning, thinking she was curled up in bed beside him.

Of course not. How stupid of him. Those days were long gone. She wasn't next to him, she was next door. There was only a single brick wall between them, but they might as well be on different planets.

Brad dragged himself out of bed and had a hot shower, but he didn't manage to scrub away the guilt and remorse. Or the sick feeling that today he was going to have to face everything he'd spent years avoiding.

Toast and coffee—thanks to the supplies Abigail had left him—made him feel more human.

OK.

He'd do the hardest bit first.

He headed into the centre of the town to renew the ticket for his parking space, then went to buy flowers. It meant he had to walk past the quay, and he could see another boat moored in the place where his father's used to be. Well, of course there would be. His mother had never really been into boats, so there was no reason for Rosie to keep the boat or the mooring after Jim's death.

But it still felt as if a little piece of his dad had been wiped away.

He bought a bunch of flowers from the shop in the middle of the high street, then walked to the church on the edge of town. It was a big old barn of a place, built of flint, with a massive tower, a lead roof and tall arched windows.

What he liked best was the inside of the church, and not just because it was full of light from those enormous windows. He turned the massive iron handle and pushed the heavy door open. He could remember coming here with his father, who'd showed him the ancient graffiti of the old-fashioned sailing ships scratched into the stone pillars, explaining they were probably prayers of thanksgiving for safe returns from long voyages.

If only James Powell had made a safe return from his last voyage.

But you couldn't change the past.

Brad shook himself and wandered through the church. There was the hexagonal stone font with its carved wooden cover and the smiling stone lions at the base—the font where he and Ruby had been christened as babies. And the ancient wooden pews with their poppyheads and carved bench ends, parts of the carvings polished smooth over the centuries where children's hands had rubbed against them. He'd always especially loved the carvings of a cat carrying one of her kittens and the mermaid.

This was the church where, if they'd waited until after his graduation, he would've married Abigail. Just as Colin would wait for Ruby on Saturday, Brad would've waited at the altar for Abby. But, because he'd been young and impetuous and desperately in love with her, he'd wanted to marry her before he went away to university. He realised now how much they'd deprived their families of a celebration. How stupid and selfish he'd been.

There were tea-light candles on a wrought-iron stand near the font, a couple of which were already lit. He lit one for his father using the wax taper provided, and stood watching the flame flicker for a while before putting some money into the slot in the wall safe.

Outside, several more graves had been dug in the churchyard since he'd last been here. And it was the first time he'd actually seen his father's headstone.

His mum had made a good choice. Together with the dates, she'd kept the words simple: *James Powell, beloved husband, father and son.* And on the back there was a carving of a boat, his father's favourite thing.

The stone vase-holder in front of the headstone was already full of flowers. Of course it would be; either Rosie or Ruby would've made sure of that. He should've thought to buy one of those pots on a spike that you could push into the earth, or bring some kind of jam jar to put his flowers in. Too late, now. He placed the wrapped bunch of flowers on the grass next to the vase, and sat cross-legged in front of the stone.

'Well. I guess it's about time I showed my face here,' he said.

Understatement of the century.

He could almost see his father's rolled eyes and hear the sarcastic comment.

'I'm sorry, Dad,' he said quietly. 'I'm sorry I couldn't save you. I'm sorry I was too far away to help.' He dragged in a breath. 'I'm sorry I've made such a mess of my life— though at least my career is doing OK. I know you were disappointed I didn't follow in your footsteps, but I would've made a lousy lawyer. I'm a good scientist. I love my job. And I think you'd approve of me being one of the youngest managers ever in the pharmaceutical company, in charge of a really big project.'

No answer. Not that he expected one. But a sudden gust of wind or an unexpected ray of sunlight would've been nice. A sign that his father had heard him.

'I'm sorry I haven't been there for Mum and Ruby,' he said. 'I wasn't trying to neglect them. It was the whole idea of coming back here. Where I'd failed you. I know, I know, I should've manned up and driven here instead of always expecting them to come and see me in London. But, the longer I stayed away, the harder it was to come home. I couldn't face walking into the house, expecting to see you and then seeing the space where you weren't there—it'd be like losing you all over again and I just couldn't bear it.'

And how he missed his father. They'd had a difficult relationship at times, but Brad had respected his father and what he'd achieved, even though they'd disagreed about Brad's career choice. James Powell was a big bear of a man, always laughing and joking, full of outrageous stories about his days in court. Brad had sneaked into the public gallery at court one day, to watch his father at work, and he'd seen how brilliant James was—persuasive, knowledgeable, putting his client's case in a way that the jury understood but without patronising them. He'd been spellbinding. A father to be proud of.

And he'd died way, way too soon.

Brad sighed. 'You were right about me and Abby. We were too young to get married. Of course it didn't last.' And how selfish he'd been to drag Abby into his teenage rebellion. If he'd waited, maybe they would still be married now. But they weren't. Another failure. Something else he hadn't wanted to face, here in Great Crowmell. The place where he'd fallen in love with Abigail Scott.

The break-up had been entirely his fault. He'd been the one to push her away.

Though seeing her again had made him realise that his old feelings for her were still there. They'd never really gone away. He'd ignored them, buried them even; but now he was home and close to her, it was harder to block them out.

He couldn't possibly act on those feelings. He didn't trust himself not to mess it all up again, and he wanted to give Abby the chance to be happy—even if it was with someone else. But maybe they could be on better terms than they'd left it last night. When she'd told him things he hadn't wanted to face and, instead of talking it over with her, he'd walked out and refused to discuss it.

'Did you ever regret things, Dad?' he asked. 'Did you ever wish you hadn't said things, or that you'd done something differently?'

Of course there was no answer.

Though his father had always been so confident, so sure that he was right.

Abby's words slid back into his head. *Your dad was a stubborn old coot. I loved Jim dearly, but he didn't help himself and he didn't listen to anyone.*

She was right; and that was probably why James had been so confident. He didn't listen to anyone who didn't say exactly what he wanted to hear. And Brad couldn't ever remember his father apologising; though Jim had come close to it in that last phone call, when he'd admitted he should've waited instead of going out on the boat on his own.

Brad sighed. 'Abby loved you. Even though you were stubborn and didn't listen to anyone except maybe your clients, she loved you.'

She'd loved Brad, too. And he'd been so sure he was right, not listening to her. Just like his father. Funny, he hadn't thought that he could be as difficult as James, but maybe he was. Being stubborn and refusing to give

up had stood him in good stead profession-
ally; the flip side meant that being stubborn
and refusing to talk about things had ruined
his marriage.

'I owe her an apology,' he said. 'For a lot
of things. I need to go and talk to her. But I'll
be back. I'll come and see you on Saturday.
And we're going to smile all day until our
faces hurt, for Ruby's sake.'

When he walked back into the florist, the
assistant raised her eyebrows. 'Back again?'

He nodded. 'Can you wrap up six roses for
me, please?' And there was only one colour
he could choose. 'Cream ones.'

'Going to see your mum now, are you?'

That was the thing about growing up in
a small town; everyone knew you, and they
knew your business, too. 'No. Actually, I'd
like a different bouquet for her, please—
something with lots of pinks and purples.'
Her favourite colours. 'Can I pick it up in an
hour? Oh, and if you have one of those vases
on a spike you can use in the churchyard, I'd
like to buy one of those, too, please.'

'Sure.'

He paid for everything, taking just the
roses and the vase with him, then bought a
bottle of water in the newsagent next door.

Then he noticed the shop next to the newsagent. Scott's Ice Cream Parlour. That was new. He'd been so focused on visiting the churchyard that he hadn't noticed it when he'd walked here before. So where would Abigail be today? Here, or at the café by the beach?

Inside, there was a young girl serving; he didn't recognise her.

'Can I help you?' she asked with a smile.

'Um, I was wondering if I could have a quick word with Abigail, please?'

'She's not here, I'm afraid. Can I take a message?'

'No, it's fine.' It looked as if he'd have to catch her at home.

'Do I hear someone asking for our Abby?' An older woman came out of the back of the shop and stared at him in surprise. 'Oh. Brad. You're back.'

'Hello, Gill.' He remembered her from the beach café, years back. 'Yes, I'm back for Ruby's wedding.'

She eyed him warily. 'I can get a message to Abby, if you like.'

It was kind of nice that Abby's staff were protective about her, he thought, not actually telling him where she was until they'd checked with her first. Though it didn't help him.

'I'm not going to fight with her,' he said

softly. 'I just wanted a quick word with her about wedding stuff.' That last bit wasn't strictly true, or anywhere even vaguely near the truth, but the first bit was heartfelt.

Gill frowned, and he thought she was going to stonewall him. But then she nodded. 'OK. It's Tuesday, so she'll be at the beach café.'

'Thank you, Gill.'

'You're welcome.' Her gaze dropped to the flowers and the vase he was carrying, and this time there was more sympathy in her expression. 'Going to see your dad?'

'Yes.' She didn't need to know it was for the second time—or that these flowers were for Abby.

'He was one of a kind, your dad. He's still missed around here.'

The words put a lump in his throat. 'Thank you.'

At the church, he sorted out the flowers he'd left at the grave earlier, pushing the spike into the earth and then filling the vase with water; then he headed for the beach café. He'd forgotten what a long walk it was from the harbour to the beach. It had always felt like seconds when he was a teenager, walking there hand in hand with Abby. Now, it seemed never-ending. And he couldn't remember the seagulls being quite so irritating and screamy, either.

Or maybe he was just out of sorts because of what he'd been doing that morning.

As he neared the café, he saw that all the tables outside were full. Dogs were sitting next to their owners or lying half under the tables; it looked idyllic. The perfect English beachside scene.

He was pretty sure that Gill would have called the café as soon as he left, so Abby would be expecting him. Hopefully she hadn't decided to leave and avoid him, or he'd have to come up with a plan B. He took a deep breath and walked inside.

She was nowhere to be seen in the café.

'Excuse me, please,' he said to the young man at the counter—someone else he didn't recognise. 'Would it be possible to have a word with Ms Scott, please?'

The young man eyed the flowers curiously.

And then it occurred to Brad that he might be causing problems for Abby if she had a new partner. A stranger bearing a bunch of roses wouldn't go down well. Even if she explained that the stranger was her ex-husband, and he was simply trying to apologise for a fight they'd had and keep things on an even keel between them for the sake of his sister's wedding.

'I'll go and get her,' the assistant said.

Abby came out from the back and he could see the second that she spotted him, because the welcome in her face turned to wariness. He sighed inwardly. It was his own fault. He'd done that with his behaviour last night.

'I know you're at work, and I don't intend to hold you up or get in the way,' he said, 'but please can I talk to you for three minutes?' And hopefully she'd realise he meant not in front of other people. He didn't want any gossip. Gossip was the thing he'd hated most about growing up in a small town.

She nodded. 'Come into the office.'

He followed her behind the counter, ignoring the curious looks from the people round them.

She closed the door of her office behind them and gestured to a chair. 'Have a seat.'

'Thank you.' He handed her the roses. 'For you.'

She frowned. 'Why?'

'A mixture of things,' he said. 'One, to say thank you for stocking my fridge.'

She lifted one shoulder in a half-shrug. 'Barely. It's what I do for all the guests next door.'

He ignored her protest. 'Two, to say thank you for sorting out the water problem. Three, to say thank you for dinner last night.' And here was the big one. 'Four, to apologise for walking out on you last night when you tried to talk to me.' He knew he owed her more than that. 'Five, to ask if you'd let me take you to dinner tonight to apologise properly—that is, if it won't cause a problem with your partner?' Because he had to face it. A woman as warm and lovely as Abigail Scott wouldn't be alone for long.

'Will it cause a problem with your partner?' she asked.

Which didn't tell him anything. Though he could hardly call her on answering a question with a question. 'I don't have a partner,' he said.

After a long, long pause, she said, 'Ditto.'

And why did that make the day feel as if the sun had suddenly come out? Crazy. He wanted Abigail to be happy. Rekindling their relationship wasn't on the cards, because he couldn't risk hurting her again. He ought to want her to have a partner instead of being alone. But a more selfish part of him was glad that she wasn't involved with anyone else.

'And six,' he said, changing the subject,

'just because five roses is an odd number. Literally and figuratively.'

That last bit made her smile, to his relief. 'Thank you. They're lovely.'

'I *am* sorry, Abby,' he said. 'I was tired and out of sorts last night, and I shouldn't have taken it out on you. I was rude, ungracious, and stubborn.'

'So only part of a chip off the old block, then,' she said.

Meaning that, unlike his father, he actually apologised? 'Maybe.' He looked her straight in the eyes. Today, they were sea green. 'Abby, I meant what I said. I'd like to take you to dinner tonight. To say thank you for looking out for me, to apologise, and to kind of cement a proper truce between us so Ruby's wedding day is perfect.'

She was silent for so long that he thought she was going to say no, but then finally she nodded. 'All right. I won't finish here until seven, though.'

'Fair enough. I'll book somewhere local for, what, eight? Will that give you enough time to be ready?' Not that Abby had ever been the high-maintenance sort who took hours and hours to get ready. Though he had no idea how much she'd changed since their divorce. Maybe she was different, now.

'That's fine,' she said.

'And I'll call for you at quarter to eight.'

She nodded. 'That'd be nice.'

'I can see you're busy,' he said, 'so I won't hold you up.'

'Thank you.'

'I'll see you tonight.'

He was at the door when she said softly, 'Brad.'

He turned round to face her. 'Yes?'

'Did you go to the church?'

He inclined his head. 'And I'm going to see Mum now.'

'That's an awful lot to face in one day.'

The quayside. The church and the church-yard. His childhood home. 'I might as well deal with most of the ghosts at once. I'll live.' It was time he stopped avoiding his past; and maybe being stubborn about it would help, for once. Doing it today would give him a couple of days' breathing space before the wedding, so he could get his mask perfect again. 'I'll see you at quarter to eight.'

Brad walked up the driveway to his parents' house—his mother's house, he corrected himself—just as he'd done so many times before. The house hadn't changed; although the paint was fresh the colour was the same and the flowers growing in the front garden were the same.

He paused with his hand on the doorbell. How many times he'd stood on this step as a teen, hoping that his dad wasn't working from home, ready with a lecture about how many more opportunities Brad would have with a law degree than with a chemistry degree. Or the row over the Cambridge college he'd applied to—not the one where James had studied. Brad had never been able to get through to his father that he loved him dearly but didn't want to follow in his footsteps; he wanted to make his own way, not trade on his father's reputation.

And now he never would.

He took a deep breath, nerving himself to ring the doorbell, when the front door opened abruptly; his mother swept him into a hug, and Ollie the Collie bounced around, barking madly.

'Brad, it's so good to have you home,' Rosie said.

Home.

'And you know you don't have to ring the doorbell. You're not a guest. This is always your home, any time you need it.'

A home with an empty space where his father should be.

Brad hugged his mother a little bit tighter, then made a fuss of the dog. 'I know, Mum.'

Her eyes were full of tears, but she blinked them away. 'It's so good to see you.'

'And you.'

She squeezed his hand. 'Last time you were here…'

She didn't need to say it. They both knew. The day of James's funeral.

'I know this is hard for you, Brad.'

It was. And her understanding made him feel worse. The lump in his throat was so huge, he could barely get the words out. 'I'm sorry, Mum. I should have come back before.'

'You video-call me twice a week and you spoil me in London. That's an awful lot more than some mothers get,' Rosie pointed out.

'I guess.' He took a deep breath. 'It's weird, being back. And it must be so hard for you—imagining Dad's going to walk in any second now.'

'I've had time to get used to it. Which isn't a criticism,' Rosie said. 'And I know your dad used to give you a hard time.'

'I let him down by not following in his footsteps.'

'You would have let me down if you'd done that,' Rosie said. 'You needed to live your own life, not relive your dad's for him. And actually he was really proud of you. I know he probably never told you, but I used to hear him talking about you to his friends. "My son, the scientist. He's going to change the world."'

'Seriously?' Brad couldn't quite square this with his memories. All the criticisms, all the witticisms, all the little digs.

'Seriously. But telling you himself would have meant admitting he was wrong, and your dad didn't do that.' Rosie raised an eyebrow. 'I thought you were heading the same way, but I'm glad you're not. I hear you've seen Abby.'

The grapevine hadn't taken long to get the news to her, he thought. 'And had a fight with her—and bought her flowers to apologise,' he said ruefully.

'But you're going to have a truce for Ruby's wedding?'

'Absolutely,' he said. 'Nothing and nobody is going to spoil my twin's special day.'

'I'm glad to hear it,' Ruby said, walking into the hall from the kitchen. 'Welcome home. It's good to see you here instead of having to trudge all the way to London.'

'You mean the place where you get free accommodation and dinner, and plenty of time to spend at exhibitions,' Brad retorted. 'Not to mention theatre tickets.'

'Yeah, yeah.' But her smile was slightly wobbly.

'I was never going to let you down,' Brad said. 'And I've been to the church. I've been to see Dad. I put flowers on his grave.'

'That's a lot of ghosts to face in one day,' Rosie said softly. 'I think you need some lunch.'

'The bread's home-made,' Ruby said. 'Though I guess we should have got you a fatted calf.'

'Except you would have made friends with it, called it "Fluffy" even if it was a fully-grown bad-tempered bull, and it would have had a regular supply of best bovine treats,' Brad said with a grin.

Ruby punched his arm. 'Not only do you look like Dad, you *sound* like him. He would've been so pleased.'

'I'm not sure whether that's a compliment or not,' Brad said. 'And I wasn't the one who kept trying to tempt you away from being a vegetarian by cooking bacon sandwiches every single day.'

'Just as well, or we would've had to call the fire brigade,' Ruby said.

And this time, when he smiled, it didn't feel forced.

'So you and Abby—you're OK?' Ruby asked.

'We're OK. Really.'

'Only I heard—'

'They're fine,' Rosie said, and hugged her daughter. 'Come on, lunch. It's good to have both my babies home.' At the look on their faces, she laughed. 'You might be twenty-seven, but I can assure you that you're still my babies. You always will be.'

'It's good to be home,' Brad said. And this time he really meant it.

CHAPTER FOUR

CREAM ROSES.

Brad had bought her cream roses.

Had he remembered that had been her wedding bouquet, Abigail wondered, a posy of half a dozen cream roses they'd bought last-minute at the local florist? Or had he just decided that roses were the best flowers to make an apology and those were the first ones he'd seen?

She raked a shaking hand through her hair. It might not have been the best idea to agree to have dinner with Brad tonight.

Then again, he'd said he wanted a truce for Ruby's sake, and they needed to talk.

But seeing him again had stirred up all kinds of emotions she'd thought she'd buried a long time ago. She'd told herself that she was over her ex and could move on. The problem was, Bradley Powell was still the most attractive man she'd ever met—those dark, dark eyes; the dark hair that she knew curled outrageously when it was wet; that sense of brooding about him. She'd never felt that same spark with anyone else she'd dated. She knew she hadn't been fair to the few men who'd asked her out; she really shouldn't have compared them to her first love, because how could they ever match up to him?

She could still remember the moment she'd fallen in love with Brad. She and Ruby had been revising for their English exams together in the garden, and Brad had come out to join them, wanting a break from his physics revision. Somehow he'd ended up reading Benedick's speeches while she'd read Beatrice's.

"'I do love nothing in the world so well as you: is that not strange?'"

She'd glanced up from her text and met his gaze, and a surge of heat had spun through her. He had been looking at her as if it were the first time he'd ever seen her. As if she were the only living thing in the world apart from himself. As if the rest of the world had just melted away…

It had felt crazy.

Abigail had known she shouldn't let herself fall for her best friend's brother. Apart from anything else, they had been way too young.

Sixteen. There had been no chance their relationship would last, and she certainly hadn't
wanted to put any strain on her friendship
with Ruby. Brad had been the last boy she
should have dated.

So she'd damped down the feelings.

But then Ruby had set him up as Abigail's
date for their school's end of year prom, the
week after their exams, on the grounds that
neither of them had had a date and she had,
and Ruby hadn't wanted either of them to
feel left out.

It had been strange. The boy she'd known
since she was a toddler, run around on the
sand with and thrown snowballs at, had suddenly been a man, in a formal suit. And the
look in his eyes when he'd seen her dressed
up in a proper long, off-the-shoulder dress—it
had been the same for him, too. Instant rec-
ognition. Shock at the changes in each other.
A realisation that they weren't kids any more:
they were grown up.

They'd danced together, and it had felt as
if she were floating. They'd danced to music
she hadn't even liked—and she really hadn't
cared, because she had been in Brad's arms.
She had barely been aware of anyone else
being in the room.

At the end of the night, he'd taken her out

into the grounds of the ancient hotel where the prom was being held and he'd kissed her among the roses. Moonlight, the scent of roses, the sound of a song thrush warbling into the night air—she would always associate those with the night Brad had first kissed her.

And from then on they'd been inseparable.

Ruby had gone to art college in September, while Brad and Abby had stayed on at their school's sixth form. And Abby had been happier than she could ever remember, spending as much time as possible with Brad. Of course she'd said yes when he'd asked her to marry him on the night of her eighteenth birthday. They'd kept their engagement secret, even from Ruby.

The original plan had been to wait until after Brad had graduated, but late one night he'd climbed up the drainpipe outside her bedroom window and said he didn't want to wait another three years to marry her. He'd suggested eloping to Gretna Green.

They'd got married in secret the week before their exam results had come out; and she'd moved to Cambridge with him when he'd started university in October.

Life had been perfect. Brad had studied while she'd worked in one of the local cafés, and they'd spent every evening and every night together. First love, true love, for ever and ever and ever. She'd been blissfully happy, and she'd thought it had been the same for Brad.

Until the weekend when she'd won a competition for a spa break.

And then everything had fallen apart.

Brad had never got over his father's death. He wouldn't talk about it, but she was pretty sure that he'd never stopped blaming himself for not being there to save his dad. And he'd built a wall of ice round himself that Abby just hadn't been able to breach. Even leaving him hadn't been enough to shock him into breaking that wall; the idea, born from sheer desperation, had blown up in her face. Brad had been supposed to realise how much he missed her and come after her and talk; instead, he'd ended their marriage completely.

Five years.

For five years she'd tried to move on.

And right now it felt as if she was back where she'd been at the start. Raw, aching, wanting a man who clearly didn't want her any more. Wanting a man who'd shattered her belief in love.

How stupid was this?

Somehow Abigail got through the rest of the day. Though those roses haunted her every time she looked up and they caught her gaze. And they haunted her even more when she went home to put them in water on her kitchen windowsill.

She had enough time to shower, change into a little black dress and reapply her make-up by the time Brad rang the doorbell.

'You look very nice,' he said.

'Thank you. So do you.' He was wearing a formal shirt and dark trousers, with perfectly polished shoes; she knew that was from his father's influence. 'So where are we going?'

'The Old Boat House,' he said.

She blinked. The restaurant in Little Crowmell, the next village round the bay, took its name from the building it had been converted from. The food was amazing—unsurprisingly, as the chef had a Michelin star—and you had to wait weeks for reservations. 'How did you manage to get a table?'

He shrugged. 'It's a Tuesday night, so I guess it's less busy than at weekends.'

It was somewhere they'd never been together—on a student budget it simply wasn't affordable—but since she'd moved back to Great Crowmell Abigail had been there with Ruby for her birthday, and a couple of times with her parents as a major treat.

She needed to remind herself that this

wasn't a *date* date. It was simply sorting things out between them and setting the terms for a truce, for Ruby's sake.

'Ready to go?' he asked.

No. She was panicking inwardly, worried that she was going to make a fool of herself over him. 'Sure,' she fibbed, trying to brazen it out.

She locked the door behind her and followed him out to his car. He didn't say much on the way to the restaurant, but put the radio on to a classical station. It suited her not to have to talk, too, and to pretend to listen to the music while her thoughts were whirring round.

Just where did they go from here? she wondered. Had he bought those roses because he too remembered their wedding day and missed the love they'd shared? Did he miss her as much as she'd missed him? Was this the first step towards repairing the bitterness of the past, maybe even trying to rekindle their lost love?

They were both older now, wiser, maybe more able to cope with life. But, if they did try again, there was no guarantee that their life together would be perfectly smooth. Unexpected things happened; the odds were that they'd hit a sticky patch. So what would happen at the next bump in their relationship? Would Brad shut her out again, just as he had when his father had died? She couldn't bear that, to make a fresh start but then go on to make exactly the same mistakes again.

Maybe it would be better to keep things between them just as friends.

And she'd tell him that tonight.

Abigail was as beautiful now as the day when he'd first fallen in love with her at their school prom, Brad thought. He'd gone as Abby's date simply as a favour to his twin, who didn't want her best friend to feel like a wallflower because Ruby was going to prom with her boyfriend. But there was something subtly different about Abby, that night. She wasn't just the girl who spent almost as much time at their house as his sister did and who felt like part of the furniture. She'd haunted him a bit since he'd read the lines from that Shakespeare play out loud and seen the wonder in her eyes, but he'd told himself that he couldn't possibly get involved with his sister's best friend. They were only sixteen, and the inevitable breakup would have too much fallout.

But at the prom he'd danced with her all night, and for him there had been nobody else in the room. Just Abby.

And then he'd taken her out into the grounds and kissed her in the middle of the rose garden. He knew at that moment that he'd met his one and only. The woman he wanted to marry. The woman he *did* marry. The woman he'd been so happy with—until he'd ruined everything.

He really didn't know where they could go from here. Maybe he could ask her to give him another chance, after Ruby's wedding. But, then again, how could he trust himself not to ruin things a second time? He was the one who'd wrecked their marriage. OK, while life was smooth, things would be absolutely fine between them; but what would happen when they hit a rocky patch? Life wasn't always perfect. Would they be strong enough as a couple to weather whatever Fate threw at them, this time round? Or would he end up letting her down again?

He didn't have the answer.

So maybe it would be better to keep things between them just as friends.

And he kind of wished he hadn't asked her out tonight. He knew they needed to talk properly and cement their truce, but all the feelings he'd once had for her had come flooding back. It was so unexpected—and it was seriously messing with his head. He really didn't know what to do. Being here with her made him feel like an awkward teenager all over again.

The same awkward teenager in a creased suit who'd married her over the anvil in Gretna Green, promising to love and cherish her for eternity...

He opened the car door for her, and she acknowledged his courtesy with a smile. His hand accidentally brushed against hers as they walked to the restaurant, and he felt a tingle through his whole body; he didn't dare look at her in case it showed in his eyes and she noticed.

What was she thinking? What was she feeling? He didn't have a clue. And asking her would break open too many things he needed to keep buried.

The *maître d'* seated them at their table with an amazing view of the sea.

'I know we won't see the actual sunset from here,' Abby said, 'but we'll still get to see the sky looking pretty, reflected in the sea.'

Not as pretty as her.

And not that Brad would be gauche enough to actually say that out loud. 'Uh-huh,' he said instead.

The waiter brought their menus over.

'Would you like wine?' Brad asked.

Abby shook her head. 'Even though I'm not officially on duty at the café again until next week, I have things to do with Ruby tomorrow, including the final dress fitting, so I'd rather keep a clear head. Still water's fine for me, please.'

He smiled at the waiter. 'Still water for both of us, please.'

He looked at the menu. 'It's been a while since I've eaten somewhere this fancy.'

She glanced at him over the top of her own menu. 'You picked it.'

'I wanted to take you somewhere nice.' And she'd mentioned it inspiring her new range of ice cream, so he'd thought she might like it here.

'It *is* nice. Thank you. I love eating here.'

When the waiter came to take their order, Brad discovered they'd both chosen the same. He should've guessed. They'd always had similar taste in food; though he'd seen food more as fuel than anything else, since she'd left.

'So how was it?' she asked.

'Which bit?'

She spread her hands. 'All of it.'

Of course she wasn't going to let him get away with fudging the issue. This was Abby.

The woman who knew him as well as he knew himself—if not better. He sighed. 'OK. Confession time. I realise now I should've come back before. I wasn't fair to Mum or to Ruby.' Or to Abby, for that matter. 'I left them to deal with it and didn't support them enough.' He'd abandoned Abby, too.

'Well, you're here now,' she pointed out. 'You're not still running away.'

Though part of him wanted to. He'd never actually told her about his clashes with Jim and how much he regretted them. He knew she was close to her own parents and he wasn't entirely sure she'd believe him, because it was so far outside her own experience. But talking about it now wouldn't change things, so he didn't tell her. Instead, he said, 'It's when you're expecting someone to walk into a room and they don't. That's the hard bit.'

She reached over the table and squeezed his hand briefly. 'I know what you mean. Every time I sit at your mum's kitchen table, I half expect your dad to walk in and ask if there's any more coffee and where are the doughnuts. It must be so much harder for you.'

'Mum says you get used to it.' He blew out a breath. 'Though I'm glad I'm staying at the cottage so I don't have to face it all day, every day.'

'That's understandable,' she said, and he was grateful that she didn't point out his mother had to face it all day, every day. 'How was the church?'

'Seeing Dad's grave was tough,' he said. 'So was walking past the quay and seeing someone else's boat in the spot where his used to be. Though of course I didn't expect Mum to keep Dad's boat. It's much better for it to have gone to someone who'll use it and enjoy it.'

'I'm glad you see it that way,' she said.

'There's no other sensible way of seeing it, and I'm not that selfish.' He hoped. Though he knew he'd already been selfish enough in the past and he needed to make amends. He needed to sort that out in his head before he talked about it, though, so he switched the subject. 'I noticed you had a new shop on the quayside.'

'The ice cream parlour. I opened it last year. It's for people who don't want to walk all the way down to the beach to get one of our ice creams,' she said, 'or maybe they just want to pick up a half-litre tub to eat at home that evening.'

'Your idea?'

'Another new direction for Scott's,' she said. 'Yes. Mum and Dad want to take it easier and—' She stopped and winced. 'Sorry. That wasn't tactful.'

'Spend time together in semi-retirement? It's what married couples of that age do,' he said. 'What my parents would've done, if Dad had been more sensible with his medication and looked after himself better instead of leaving it all to Mum.'

She said nothing, simply looked at him.

'You were right,' he said softly. 'Everything you said about Dad, last night. He was stubborn, he didn't listen to anyone—and I really ought to learn from his mistakes.'

'Does that include looking after yourself better, rather than spending twice as many hours as you ought to in the lab and living off sandwiches and microwave meals?' she asked.

It was how he got by.

But he was saved from answering by the arrival of their first course: heritage tomato salad with pesto and burrata, all soft and wobbly and creamy.

'This is fabulous,' he said.

He managed to keep the conversation going about food during the second course, too: monkfish wrapped in Parma ham, served on a bed of lentils with samphire, plus a cauliflower and saffron purée.

'I'm a bit disappointed not to see your Parmesan ice cream on the menu today,' he said to Abigail after the waiter brought the dessert menu.

'If you really want to try it, I can always make you some,' she said. 'It was very popular in the eighteenth century. Though one glass of ice cream cost about the same as the average daily wage, so really it was only for the super-rich.'

'Have you thought about making historic recipes?' he asked. He remembered she'd always loved history. It had been her favourite A level subject.

'I do sometimes. I have an ancient brown bread ice cream recipe. But I'm experimenting with a few "free-from" options at the moment. Mum's been diagnosed as having coeliac disease, so that led me to source gluten-free wafers. And I've been making non-dairy ice cream with oat milk or almond milk for people who have dairy allergies. Or vegans—you know Ruby's thinking about taking the next step from being a vegetarian.'

He didn't. And he felt another twinge of guilt that he really hadn't paid enough attention to his sister.

'She's my main beta tester.' Abigail smiled. 'I get people to fill in comment cards in the shop and the café, too—if they do, they go in a monthly draw to win a voucher for Scott's. Plus then I have their details for our mailing list when we release a new product.'

He wasn't surprised that Abigail had moved the business forward. Or that she'd turned out to be a savvy, thoughtful business-woman. That had been so obvious in their Cambridge years; she'd been bubbling over with ideas and it was easy to see that she had what it took to grow Scott's. Only now he was seeing that potential actually realised, and it was a bit of a jolt to see that the naive, shy teenager he'd married was now well on the way to becoming a tycoon.

'And everything I sell is made from local ingredients, as much as possible,' she said. 'The local dairy supplies my dairy products; the farm shop supplies my fruit and veg; I have an arrangement with the local fishmon-ger and butcher; my flour's stone-ground from a local watermill—actually, they sup-ply my bread as well—and even my coffee's roasted locally.'

'That's impressive,' he said.

'I want to make a difference,' she said. 'Yes, it's a little bit more expensive than using the cash and carry supermarket, and my prices reflect that—but my customers know that when they buy from me they're supporting local businesses and reducing their carbon footprint. And that's important to them as well as to me.'

He could just see Abigail being named local businessperson of the year. And he was proud of the woman she'd become: bright, confident and with a huge heart. The woman he'd always known she'd become. The woman he missed so very much…

Not that he could tell her that. He didn't have the right. Not any more.

'It sounds as if you're really settled. Though I'm guessing the hours you work are ridiculous.'

She shrugged. 'I don't mind. I love it here. I love the café, I love my staff, and I love Great Crowmell.'

Which was a timely warning for him. He didn't love it here. He didn't love the town, he didn't want to come back here, and his job was in London. There was no room for compromise, not when they lived three hours apart. That would be way too much of a commute for either of them.

So keeping things polite and a little bit distant would be the best the two of them could do. As for that weird yearning: he'd just have to try and bury it until he was back in London.

He managed to make polite conversation until the end of the meal, and then drove her back to Great Crowmell. Even if he hadn't hired the cottage next door to hers, he would've walked her home—his father had impressed the importance of good manners on him.

'Goodnight,' he said outside her front door, and leaned forward to kiss her on the cheek. Just to prove to both of them that they could do this—that they would be fine around each other at the wedding.

Except somehow his lips didn't meet her cheek.

Instead, they brushed against her lips. Very gently. Very lightly.

It felt as if he'd been burned.

But, instead of backing away sensibly, he found himself kissing her again. Then he drew back far enough to look her straight in the eye.

Sea green.

Not grey.

And her lips were parted very, very slightly. Inviting him. Telling him that it was the same for her—that right at this second she wanted them to kiss, too.

Memories collided in his head. The first time he'd kissed her, in the moonlight among the roses. The first time he'd kissed her before making love. Kissing her over the anvil in Gretna Green, their first kiss as a married couple.

How he'd missed her.

How he wanted her.

And he couldn't help leaning forward again. This time, she let him deepen the kiss, sliding her hands round the back of his neck and twining her fingers in his hair. And he wrapped his arms round her, holding her close, feeling the thud of her heartbeat—just as she must be feeling the thud of his.

Her mouth was so soft. So sweet. And it felt as if every nerve end in his body had just burst into life after five years of being dormant.

Shaking, he broke the kiss, and they stared at each other.

That really, really wasn't supposed to happen, Abigail thought. Right now Brad was more off limits than he'd ever been. It was Ruby's wedding in four days' time and they were supposed to be keeping a truce, not trying to rekindle the past. She was supposed to be telling him that they could be friends and nothing else.

But the way he'd just kissed her had blown her mind.

His hands were still splayed on her back and her hands were still loosely round his neck. Right now, they were like the teenagers they'd once been, kissing in a doorway.

And she felt just as she had the first time he'd ever kissed her, in that rose garden. Light-headed, needing to hold on to him to stop herself falling over.

This was a really bad idea.

They needed to stop.

Now.

She slid her hands back from his neck and took one step backwards, not quite trusting herself to stand upright, but thankfully that one step meant she could lean against her front door. And he clearly felt the same way that she did—spooked by the strong sensual reaction between them and not knowing what to do—because he stopped holding her, but he didn't move from where he was.

What now?

It would be oh, so easy to step forward again, kiss him and lead him upstairs to her bedroom. But she knew it would be a hideous mistake and they'd both regret it in the morning. They couldn't go back. Shouldn't go back.

'I...' Her voice sounded cracked to her own ears.

'We shouldn't,' he said, his own voice sounding just as hoarse.

'We have a truce. For Ruby's sake.' She forced the words out. 'And we'll be polite and civil to each other.'

'Agreed.'

'I'm going to bed now,' she said. When she realised that it sounded like an invitation, she added, 'Alone.' And her voice *would* have to squeak on that word, wouldn't it?

'Me, too,' he said. Though his expression said otherwise. The heat in his eyes told her he wanted to repeat their wedding night, to carry her over the threshold of their bedroom and then make slow, sweet love to her until they were both dizzy.

But they couldn't go back.

They *couldn't.*

'Goodnight,' she said, and turned away. While she still had the strength to do it.

Brad couldn't sleep. When the early-morning light poured in through the thin cotton curtains, he gave up trying, pulled on some clothes and a pair of running shoes, and went for a run to clear his head. It was early enough that the streets were mostly deserted—too early for anyone to go into the town to pick up a news-paper or a pint of milk before rushing to work. He'd forgotten how steep and narrow some of the back streets were, sloping up away from the harbour, and he'd worked up a decent sweat by the time he got back to the cottage. Which would have to be at exactly the same time that Abigail, also dressed in running gear, got back to the front door of her own cottage.

He could make this awkward.

Or he could keep it light and pretend that the kiss last night never happened.

It might be cowardly; but it might also be kinder to both of them.

'Fancy seeing you here,' he said.

'Anyone would think we lived near each other,' she said wryly. 'Temporarily.'

'Do you go running every morning?' he asked, suddenly curious. She'd never really been one for sport when they'd been together, preferring to curl up with a book or listen to music. That was another area where she'd changed.

'Yes. It clears my head and sets me up for work. Well, not that I'm at work today, but it's a good habit.' She looked at him. 'You?'

'Same.'

This was his cue to smile, say good morning, and walk inside.

But his mouth clearly wasn't with the programme. 'Maybe we could have lunch.'

'Sorry. I've got a final dress fitting with Ruby and Izzy.'

'Izzy?' It wasn't a name he knew. The dressmaker, perhaps?

'Isabella. Colin's niece—the other bridesmaid. She's seven years old and very sweet.'

Ruby had probably already told him and he hadn't been paying attention. Guilt twisted through him again.

And that was her cue to say good morning and walk away. Except her mouth clearly wasn't with the programme, either, because she said, 'Maybe we could grab some fish and chips tonight.'

'And eat them on the harbour wall.' Like tourists, or like the teenagers they'd once been. He liked that idea. 'What time?'

'How about seven o'clock?'

'That's fine. I'll knock for you.' He smiled. 'Have a good day.'

'You, too.'

At seven precisely, Brad knocked on Abigail's front door.

'Hi.' She was wearing faded jeans and a T-shirt, and no make-up.

'How was the dress fitting?'

'Fine,' she said. 'How was your day?'

'Fine. I spent most of it with Mum.'

'But you sneaked in some work?' she asked.

He smiled. 'As if you didn't.'

'I ticked a few things off my to-do list,' she admitted with a grin. 'My staff are great, but I don't want to take unfair advantage of them and dump my responsibilities on them.'

'Same here,' he said. 'I never used to understand what you meant about getting to know your team and developing them, when we were in Cambridge. I do now.'

'So you like managing a team?'

'As part of a project, yes. Watching their confidence grow and knowing I've helped that—it's a good feeling.' Something else they had in common, now.

They walked to the fish and chip shop and bought cod and chips, then ate them out of the cardboard box with a wooden fork while sitting on the harbour wall.

'Remember doing this, years ago?' he asked.

She nodded. 'And sitting on the dunes on the beach, watching the stars come out.'

'Star light, star bright…' And he thought, that the wish he'd make now wasn't achievable because the past couldn't be changed. 'We could do that now.'

She blinked. 'What?'

'Go and sit on the dunes and watch the stars,' he said.

She was silent for long enough that he thought she was going to refuse, but then she nodded. 'OK.'

When they'd finished their meal, they walked all the way from the harbour to the dunes. They didn't talk on the way there but it was an easy silence, not an awkward one. Especially as their hands had brushed against each other and their fingers had ended up entwined; he didn't want to say anything to break the spell, and he guessed it was the same for her.

And he couldn't get that kiss from last night out of his head. Had it been a mistake? Or had it been one step closer towards changing things between them? Towards making things better?

They sat on the dunes, still holding hands, just listening to the swish of the sea and watching the sky change colour; the band of deep purple at the horizon shaded up to pink, apricot and finally to blue.

'Look, it's the first star.' She pointed up to it with her free hand. 'Though I know it's a planet, not a star, because it doesn't twinkle. I remember you telling me that.'

He remembered that evening, too. 'It's Jupiter.'

She smiled. 'Trust you to know that.'

He gave a half-shrug. 'I don't see the stars much in London.' And that was one thing he missed about Great Crowmell. Out here, they were far enough away from the town for the sky not to be so affected by the light pollution. 'Every so often, I see news reports about sightings of the Northern Lights out here.'

'And every time I see those reports, Ruby and I gnash our teeth,' she said. 'We always manage to miss them, even though I get email alerts from the university about when a sighting's possible.'

He knew that was top of her bucket list, seeing the aurora borealis. He'd always intended to take her to the Arctic Circle, the winter after he'd finished his doctorate, so she could see them. Except life had changed unimaginably before then. The winter after he'd finished his doctorate, they'd already been divorced for a long, long time.

Trying to keep things light, he pointed out some of the constellations to her.

Even though it was summer, the night was still cool; he loosened his fingers from hers and slid his arm round her. 'Because it's cold,' he said. 'And, scientifically speaking, sharing body heat is the most efficient way of keeping warm.'

It was true, on a superficial level; but he knew it wasn't the real reason why he'd put his arm round her. He'd wanted to be close to her. And she hadn't moved away...

Then he looked at her. Her eyes were huge and her mouth was slightly parted.

What else could he do but kiss her, here under the stars, with the sea swishing gently in the background?

When he broke the kiss, he whispered, 'I'm sorry. For so very much.'

'It wasn't all you,' she said.

He didn't deserve this kindness, and his heart broke a little more. 'We were young. I handled everything badly. And I'm truly sorry I hurt you so much.'

'Apology accepted.'

He noticed that she didn't say it was all right. Because it wasn't all right. The past couldn't be changed.

But the fact she'd accepted his apology meant that perhaps they could both move on instead of being stuck.

'You have wedding stuff to do with Ruby tomorrow,' he said. 'We'd better head back.'

He resisted the urge to kiss her again.

Though, when he offered her his hand to help her to her feet, he didn't let her hand go until they were outside the row of cottages.

It would be oh, so easy to ask her to come in. To stay with him tonight.

But that wouldn't be fair. He couldn't offer her a future. And he'd let her down before.

Instead, he brushed his mouth against hers. Lightly. Not demanding. 'Goodnight, Abby. Sleep well.'

And he unlocked his door and went inside before he did anything stupid—like picking her up and carrying her over the threshold.

Abby let herself indoors and curled up on the sofa.

That kiss yesterday had blown all her defences wide apart.

And tonight, eating fish and chips with him on the harbour wall and then going to the dunes to watch the stars come out—it was like reliving the best bits of their teenage courtship.

The worst thing was, she realised she was more than halfway to falling in love with Brad all over again. If she'd ever actually fallen out of love with him. Which she was really beginning to doubt.

She needed to get herself under control. He

wasn't going to stay here, and this was where she belonged. They couldn't have a future together. Their lives had gone off at tangents from each other, and there was no way they could compromise.

At least she'd be busy for the next couple of days with Ruby, too busy to spend any time with Brad. She'd keep herself under rigid control at the wedding, making sure she was polite but keeping a distance between them. And then, after the wedding, he'd leave again—and she would have time to bring herself properly back to her senses.

CHAPTER FIVE

SATURDAY DAWNED BRIGHT and sunny: perfect weather for a wedding.

As the stand-in for the father of the bride, officially Brad didn't have anything much to do before the wedding apart from getting dressed and then accompanying Ruby to the church. But he knew exactly what James Powell would've done. He would've shooed his wife out of the kitchen and told Rosie to get ready with the girls, and he would've been the one dispensing cups of tea and terrible jokes and lots of hearty laughter.

Well, Brad could do that. Maybe not the hearty laughter and terrible jokes, because he wasn't a showman like his father had been; but he could do tea and calmness.

Colin was staying overnight with his brother Richard, mindful of all the old wives' tales about not seeing the bride on the morning of the wedding until she walked down the aisle. Brad and Abigail had got dressed together; maybe that had been one of the first in a long line of mistakes. Along with not having something old, something new, something borrowed and something blue, he thought.

He shook himself. Today wasn't about himself and Abby—or the fact that she'd managed to avoid him ever since the night they'd sat and watched the stars come out and kissed each other. They'd be polite and civil to each other today, and maybe they could talk tomorrow.

He made mugs of tea for his mother, sister, Abby and Isabella's mother Sadie, and added a glass of milk for Isabella, then took the tray upstairs and knocked on Ruby's door. 'I'm leaving a tray of tea outside,' he said. 'By the way, the wedding flowers are here and they all look perfect. And there was an extra delivery for you, Ruby.'

A single deep red rose, with a message from Colin—no doubt telling her how much he loved her and how he was looking forward to marrying her later that day. Yeah. Brad remembered that feeling. How excited he'd been, hardly able to wait for the rest of his life to start—his new life as Abby's husband.

Older, wiser, he reminded himself. And divorced.

He dispensed bacon rolls—a hummus and falafel wrap, in his sister's case—mid-morning; and dispensed more tea when the hairdresser and make-up artist arrived.

And then finally it was time to head for the church.

Ruby emerged in a gorgeous strapless lacy gown, her hair in an updo and a tiara securing her veil. Brad had a lump in his throat as he looked at her. 'You look amazing. Dad would've been so proud of you.' He hugged her, careful not to crease her dress or spoil her make-up. 'You look fabulous, too, Mum.'

'Thank you,' Ruby and Rosie chorused.

'And you, Isabella. You look very pretty.'

But the one who really made his jaw drop was Abby. She looked stunning in a deep red dress with a V-neck and tiny shoulder straps; it was fitted at the waist and fell to the floor. And he knew every curve under that dress, knew every inch of skin. The memory practically poleaxed him.

What did he say to her?

His throat dried.

Polite and civil. That was what they'd agreed. He didn't dare meet her eye, and he drew on every reserve he had to make sure he didn't give a keynote speech worthy of a conference. 'You look very nice, too, Abigail.'

'Thank you,' she said, her tone equally polite and civil.

Had she guessed at how much his thoughts were churning? He hoped not. 'The cars are here,' he said.

He made sure that his mother, Abigail, Isabella and Sadie were all comfortably seated, then helped Ruby into their own car.

'Thank you,' Ruby said when he'd closed the door. 'You and Abby—I have to admit, I did worry a bit. Especially as she's been very quiet about you.'

So obviously Abby hadn't said a word to his twin about the kisses they'd exchanged. Or maybe they'd put her in as much of a spin as they'd done to him, and that was why she'd used the excuse of chief bridesmaid's duties to avoid him for the last couple of days. Not wanting to make today difficult, he'd backed off. 'It's fine,' he said. 'We're fine.' Even though they weren't, they *would* be for today. He'd make sure of that. Ruby's wedding wasn't going to be collateral damage from any problems between himself and Abby.

'I wish Dad was here,' Ruby said, a slight crack in her voice.

'Me, too.' He took her hand. 'But I'm pretty sure he's here in spirit. And he'd really love the woman you've become.' He looked at her. 'Don't cry. Mum and Abby will kill me if your make-up's even the slightest bit smudged.'

Ruby blinked hard. 'I won't cry.'

'Be happy, Rubes,' he said. And he wanted her to be as happy as he and Abby had been at the start of their own married life. Except he wanted that happiness to last for his sister for ever. 'Colin's a good man and I like him very much. But I know what Dad would be saying to you right now, and because he can't say it then it's my job to say it for him. I love you, and if you've got even the slightest, tiniest doubt about marrying Colin then you don't have to walk down that aisle today. I'll sort everything out for you so you won't have to worry. Nothing matters except that you're happy.'

'I don't have any doubts. I want to get married to Colin.' Ruby looked straight at him. 'Did you have any doubts when you married Abby?'

The question felt like a sucker-punch to his gut. He'd never told anyone why he'd rushed Abby off to Gretna Green—not even Abby herself. 'No. But don't repeat my mistakes, OK?'

His sister regarded him narrowly. 'Are you sure you're going to be OK with all this?'

'It's your wedding day. Of course I'm sure,' he said. 'You're going to have a lovely wedding and a lovely life with a man who adores you.'

She squeezed his hand. 'Love you, Brad. And I wish…'

'Yeah. Me, too.' He wished a lot of things. That his dad were still there. That he hadn't shut Abby out. That he could find some compromise to suit them both.

He couldn't change the past. But could he change their future?

At the church, he helped Ruby out of the car. Abigail straightened Ruby's veil and made sure she was ready for the first batch of photographs.

And then it was time to walk down the aisle.

This service would be a much happier occasion than the last one he'd attended here.

To the sound of Pachelbel's *Canon*—one of their father's favourite pieces of music, and he knew that was why Ruby had chosen it—he walked his twin down the aisle and gave her away to Colin in the middle of the ceremony. But when he took his place in the pew for the rest of the service, he wasn't looking at the bride and groom; he only had eyes for the chief bridesmaid. She looked wistful.

Was it just the way women always looked at weddings—or was she thinking of their own wedding, right now, the way that he was? Remembering all the tiny details, all the little things that had made that day so special?

After Ruby and Colin signed the register and walked back down the aisle, there was a blur of photographs.

Brad chose that moment to sneak away to visit Jim's grave. 'I hope I did you proud today, Dad,' he said softly. 'Ruby looks so happy. I wish you were here with us, but I'll raise a glass to you later.'

Once the photographer was happy she'd got the shots she wanted, everyone headed to the big gorgeous hotel on the edge of town, which had once been the local mansion. The reception was being held in the former ballroom; the places were all immaculately set with silver and fine china and crystal glasses, and there were fresh flowers on every table.

Ruby's table arrangements were a little unconventional, though Brad was relieved he wasn't sitting near Abby—or anywhere near where he could see her and be distracted. Right now, he was focusing on making his sister's day as perfect as it could be, and he knew that Abby was doing the same. Having to face each other would complicate things.

His was the first speech after the meal, in the place of the bride's father. 'I'd like to thank everyone for coming and to welcome you to Ruby and Colin's wedding,' he said. 'And I'd also like to make a toast to our dad, who I'm sure is with us in spirit. I have to admit, I'm finding his shoes pretty hard to fill and I'm not going to do the kind of witty speech that he would've done—I'm going to keep it short and simple. But what I do know is that Dad would've been so proud of the wonderful woman my sister has become, just as I am. I'd like to welcome Colin to our family and it's good to have a new brother. In fact, it's rather nice to have another Y chromosome around to even things up a little in our family.'

Everyone duly laughed, and he relaxed. 'I give you the bride and groom, Ruby and Colin.'

'Ruby and Colin,' everyone echoed.

Colin made a speech about how much he loved his new wife that had a lump in everyone's throat; and then Richard, his brother, lightened things up again by telling the traditional best man's funny stories about the groom.

Then Ruby stood up. 'I'd like to say a big thank you to everyone for coming,' she said. 'And to my twin, Brad, for standing in for

Dad today—and Dad would've been just as proud of our brilliant scientist, too. To Colin, for making me happier than I've ever known. To Mum, for being the best support ever. To Izzy, for being the greatest flower girl. And especially to Abby, because I could never have organised this without my best friend. We've known each other since we were toddlers and I love her like a sister. Please raise your glasses to my chief bridesmaid and ice cream maker extraordinaire, the woman behind the ice creams you'll all be eating in the garden this afternoon, Abigail Scott.'

Guilt flickered through Brad. Abby *had* been Ruby's sister—well, sister-in-law—until he'd messed everything up. But he was glad their friendship hadn't become collateral damage in the divorce.

Somehow he and Abby were both too busy with wedding details to speak to each other for the rest of the afternoon; she was supporting her staff at the old-fashioned ice cream cart and checking if there was anything they needed, and he was making sure that everyone had a drink.

Finally, it was time for the evening reception and the DJ announced the first dance; Ruby and Colin walked onto the dance floor together to George Michael's cover of 'The

First Time Ever I Saw Your Face' and began a slow, sweet waltz.

The words of the song were so perfect; and they made Brad think of Abby. Unable to help himself, he glanced over the other side of the ballroom at her—to see that she was looking right back at him.

Was she thinking the same that he was?

Polite and civil, he reminded himself. That was the order of the day. Polite and civil. He could absolutely not be a troglodyte and scoop up the chief bridesmaid, haul her over his shoulder and carry her off to his lair. Particularly as his cottage was a couple of miles down the road. And particularly as lots of their family and friends were there to witness everything and he was very aware of the speculative glances.

Plus it was time for the traditional father-daughter dance. He couldn't help smiling as the music Ruby had chosen came on: ABBA's 'Dancing Queen'. It was the song she and Abby claimed would get anyone up on a wedding dance floor. Colin was dancing with his mother, Frances. Then they swapped round and Colin danced with his new mother-in-law, Rosie, while Ruby danced with Jeremy, Colin's dad; and Richard, Colin's brother, was dancing with Abby.

'Don't you dare try to sneak off this dance floor,' Ruby warned Brad as she passed him.

'As if I would,' Brad fibbed. But he was dreading the moment when he knew he was supposed to dance with Abby. How could he keep things polite and civil, when his emotions were raging inside him? That sense of loss and regret, knowing it was all his own fault and wishing things were different, wishing he had the right to hold her close and remember their own wedding day and kiss her under the stars…

The rest of the guests joined in and the DJ kept things upbeat for a while, getting all the generations doing their particular versions of dances to wedding classics.

'I guess the chief bridesmaid and the bride's brother ought to dance,' Abby said, coming to stand next to him. 'Before the bride starts fretting that they're having a fight.'

Polite and civil, he reminded himself. They could do this. 'Sure,' he said lightly.

He was expecting another upbeat song, one he could cope with—but, to his shock, the DJ chose that precise moment to dim the lights and slow things down with an old, old slow song.

They could hardly back out of it now, not without making a scene and making everyone feel awkward.

But dancing close to her like this…

Especially to this song. Art Garfunkel's 'I Only Have Eyes for You'—it was horribly appropriate. Because right now, there was nobody else in the room for him. Was it the same for her?

Maybe it was because, when the song ended and he forced himself to break the dance hold and take a step backwards from her, she looked as dazed as he felt.

Thankfully Stuart, her father, stepped in to dance with her; and Rosie came to dance with Brad.

'That was a lovely speech you made, darling,' she said.

'It's a lovely wedding, Mum,' he said, smiling at her.

'It is.' Rosie looked slightly anxious. 'Do you mind about George being at the wedding?'

'George?'

She looked pained. 'I told you about George earlier in the week.'

Of course. Her new partner. The one Brad hadn't met because George's elderly and frail mother had been taken ill last weekend, and George had gone to be with her. He'd come back today for the wedding, and Brad had shaken hands with him this afternoon and made polite and anodyne conversation.

How could he have forgotten? The emotion of the wedding—and of dancing with Abby—must've pushed it all out of his head.

But he really appreciated the fact George hadn't tried to take Jim's place on the day. He'd been diffident and decent and kept in the background, near enough to support Rosie but without pushing himself forward. He was a good man. And, most importantly, Brad liked the way that George looked at his mother.

'Mum, I want you to be happy,' Brad said.

'I know how badly you took your dad's death. I wasn't sure how you'd react to the idea of me seeing someone else. I've wanted to tell you about George for the last year,' Rosie said. 'I should've told you before this week.'

Except he'd made himself unavailable. Been utterly selfish. Maybe Abby was right about that hair shirt. 'I wish you had told me about him before,' he said. 'It would've been nice to meet him sooner and get to know him properly.' And he meant it.

'So you really don't mind that I'm dating someone?'

'Mum, you're not exactly wizened and ancient. You can't be on your own for the rest of your life,' he said. 'Dad wouldn't have wanted that for you either. He loved you enough to want you to be happy, not being a—a—' He struggled to find the right words. 'A Miss Havisham.'

'Wrong character, darling. Miss Havisham was a jilted bride, not a widow,' Rosie pointed out with a smile.

'I'm a scientist, not an English Lit graduate,' he reminded her, smiling back. 'You know what I mean, Mum. Isolating yourself and being miserable and living in the past. That's not what any of us wants for you, and Dad wouldn't have wanted that either. George seems a nice guy, Ruby likes him, and if he treats you the way you deserve then that's good enough for me.'

She hugged him. 'Thank you.'

'It's Ruby's special day,' he said. 'I want her to be happy—and I want you to be happy, too.'

'I am, but I worry about you. So does Ruby.' Rosie looked at him. 'I saw you dancing with Abby earlier.'

'We're both adults. We can be civil to each other,' he said mildly. Even though 'civil' didn't even begin to cover the complexity of his feelings towards her.

'She's still part of our family,' Rosie said.

'She's Ruby's best friend. Of course she's

part of the family.' Even though she wasn't still married to him.

'She's not just Ruby's best friend. I still think of Abby as a daughter and I love her dearly. I just wish…' Rosie broke off and sighed.

'I know, Mum.' He hugged her. 'But you can't change the past. Now, go and dance with George, and let me get you both a glass of champagne first.'

Abby was dancing with someone he didn't know, someone who was clearly attracted to her by the way he was holding her. Jealousy flickered through him. And how bad was it that, when she didn't accept a second dance, he was pleased about it?

He ought to let her move on. Find someone else. Hadn't that been the whole reason he'd walked away from their marriage, to give her a chance to find happiness?

The problem was, his twin's wedding had brought back so many memories of his own.

Of dancing with Abby in their room on their wedding night, with music playing on his phone.

Of making love with her…

He managed to keep his distance for a full hour and a half.

But then another slow song came on. 'Moon

River.' The song he'd always associated with Abby's favourite Audrey Hepburn movie and it made him itch to hold her. Before he knew what he was doing, he was right by her side.

'Might I have this dance, Ms Scott?'

'Sure.' She gave him a polite, civil smile.

But the dance wasn't polite and civil at all. They moved closer and closer together until their feet were barely moving and they were just swaying together; her heels were high enough that all he had to do was dip his head slightly and he could press his cheek to hers.

And how good it felt to be cheek to cheek with her. Holding her close. Feeling the warmth of her skin against his, the regular thud of her heartbeat.

But this time he was all too aware of the people around him. Right now, he wanted to be alone with her. Find out what was going on in her head.

'Do you want to go and get some fresh air?' he whispered in her ear.

'Good idea,' she whispered back.

He broke the dance hold and just about stopped himself taking her hand, but they walked out together into the garden. There were fairy lights strung all round the garden through the trees and shrubs, creating a soft warm glow in the twilight. The romance of the garden was intensified even more by the roses, where all the blooms were out and it felt as if they were breathing nothing but the sweet scent of them.

They'd been here before. A different function and a different garden, but it felt the same. The same as the night they'd first got together at their school prom.

He could hear the music from the ballroom, another slow song.

'Dance with me here?' he asked.

And it was just as if the years had melted away, as they held each other in the light of the moon and the fairy lights. Dancing cheek to cheek.

Except this time he moved so he could kiss the corner of her mouth.

And she responded by twisting slightly to brush her lips properly against his.

And then they were really kissing, holding onto each other as if to save each other from drowning in the sudden sea of emotion that threatened to swamp them both.

When he broke the kiss, he was shaking and her pupils were enormous.

He stroked her cheek. 'This reminds me of prom. The day when I really noticed you for the first time.'

'So before then I was just your sister's annoying friend?'

He smiled. 'No. I always liked you. But that time in the garden when I helped you and Ruby revise your Shakespeare—I felt something different, then. I knew I shouldn't get involved with you because you were my sister's best friend, and that made you off limits.'

'But you let her fix us up on a date for prom, a few weeks later,' she pointed out.

'I did it as a favour to Ruby. She was worried that you'd be a wallflower.'

'She told me she was worried that you wouldn't have a date because you were the biggest nerd in the world,' she countered.

'She was right. I was. I probably still am,' he said. He laughed, and stole a kiss. 'Abby. Today. We're supposed to be polite and civil to each other.'

'So why are we alone in the garden together? Why did you kiss me?'

'And why did you kiss me back?' he asked.

'I...' She shook her head, as if unable to find the words.

'Maybe it's just the emotion of the wedding.' He knew that he was lying. He was here because he wanted to be here. He'd kissed Abby because he'd wanted to kiss her. Because he couldn't help himself.

'It's a good wedding.'

He nodded. 'And it's made me realise how selfish we were, eloping the way we did.'

'We were so young,' she said. 'Just eighteen.'

'And we didn't think of anything or anyone else,' he said. 'Just Gretna Green.'

She wrinkled her nose. 'We deprived everyone of a good party.'

'But I never, ever regretted marrying you,' he said.

She looked straight at him. 'So why did you divorce me?'

The big question. And he owed her honesty. 'Because I thought I was doing the right thing.'

She rolled her eyes. 'Are you trying to tell me there was a shiny suit of armour on top of that hair shirt of yours, and you were riding a white horse at the time?'

'Abby, I was a mess. I felt I was dragging you down.'

'That's the point of wedding vows, for better or worse. We should've stuck it out,' she said.

She could say that now? 'You were the one who left me,' he pointed out.

'I wasn't deserting you when you needed me.'

'It felt like it, though.'

'I simply wanted to shock you into realising what you were doing and stop you pushing me away all the time.' Her eyes filmed with tears. 'But it backfired. You divorced me. It wasn't supposed to be like that.'

He hadn't wanted the divorce, either. He'd wanted Abby—but he'd tried so hard to be unselfish, to unshackle her from the mess he knew he'd become so she would have a chance to be happy. 'It's nearly five years.' He rested his palm against her cheek.

She turned into it, kissing his palm, and it felt as if he'd been galvanised. 'And neither of us has really moved on, have we?'

No. They hadn't. That was a problem they needed to solve, because they couldn't go on like this.

Though there was a solution. An insane one. She might say no if he suggested it, and he'd accept that. Then again, she might say yes. And how he wanted her to say yes. His heart thumping, he said, 'Maybe we need closure. To get things out of our system at last.'

'Closure. Getting things out of our system. Maybe you're right.' Her eyes were sea green. 'The bride and groom have slipped off to their honeymoon suite. We don't have to be here any more.'

So she was thinking along the same lines that he was? 'We could get a taxi. Go…' No. It wasn't home. Nowhere had felt like home since she left him. Not the flat they'd shared, not the college rooms he'd moved into after the divorce, not the flat he'd bought when he'd accepted the job in London. 'Back to the cottage,' he finished.

She was silent for so long that he thought she'd changed her mind. But then she nodded. 'I'll text my mum and say I'm fine but I have a bit of a headache and I'm going home for an early night, so nobody worries about me.'

He stole a kiss. 'Good thinking. I'll do the same.'

And from there it was easy.

A taxi was there in five minutes.

They didn't say a word to each other all the way back to the centre of town. They didn't need to. He paid the taxi driver, unlocked the door and ushered her inside.

'Coffee?' he asked.

'That'd be nice.'

While the kettle was boiling, he switched on some music then held out his hand to her. 'Dance with me?'

She took his hand and let him draw her into his arms. They swayed together, and when his mouth found hers the rest of the world felt a million miles away.

Coffee forgotten, he carried her up the stairs to his bed. Unzipped her dress and hung it neatly over the back of a chair, then let her strip off his tailcoat and waistcoat.

'Nice,' she said when she'd undone his tie and shirt, then ruffled his hair and grinned. 'You always did look sexy when you came home from the lab, all dishevelled because you'd stuck your hands through your hair like an absent-minded professor while you were thinking about a problem and it never occurred to you to look in a mirror or comb your hair before you came home.'

She remembered? Warmth spread through him.

'And you've always been the sexiest woman I've ever known,' he said, his voice husky with longing.

'Yeah?'

'Yeah. The day we got married. Me in that crumpled suit and you in that pretty summer dress.'

'You and me, always. That's what we said. And it didn't happen.' Her eyes filled with sadness.

He kissed her. 'Let's remember the good

stuff, not the bad.' The beginning of their marriage, all those years ago.

And maybe tonight would be closure.

Closure on all the hurt and pain between them.

A chance to move on.

And maybe tomorrow the future would look bright instead of bleak.

CHAPTER SIX

ABIGAIL HALF OPENED her eyes as the light filtered through the curtains.

Then she was instantly awake.

Her own curtains had blackout linings. These ones didn't—because they weren't her curtains. This wasn't her bed. And the man spooned against her, with one arm wrapped round her waist holding her close to him, hadn't slept in the same bed as her for nearly five years.

Oh, help.

Had this just been the worst mistake of her life?

Maybe it was the wedding that had got to her; it had brought back memories of her own wedding day and how happy she and Brad had been. And it had been, oh, so easy to fall into his arms yesterday. To kiss him in the garden. To let him carry her to his bed when they'd caught a taxi back to his cottage.

She had absolutely no idea what would happen today. They'd both said they needed closure, but had this been the wrong way to do it? There hadn't been any kind of closure when they'd got divorced. The whole process had all been cold and distant, done through their respective solicitors, and it had left her with so many unanswered questions. Had she not been enough for Brad in the first place, that he'd let her go so easily? Or should she have tried harder to fight for her marriage?

Maybe she ought to leave. But right now she was warm and comfortable, with his arms wrapped round her, and she didn't want to go anywhere.

How stupid was she, trying to cling on to the past?

They couldn't go back. She knew that.

But making love with Brad again hadn't got him out of her system. At all. If anything, it had made her realise just how much she missed him. She filled her life with work—and she loved her business, her staff and her life here—but she knew perfectly well that she kept herself busy to stave off the loneliness. And, although she'd dated a few men during those years, nobody had ever managed to make her feel even the tiniest bit the way Bradley Powell had. So the fairest thing to do had been to keep all her relationships platonic and just not bother dating.

But what now?

How would Brad feel, when he woke?

Would he think last night was a huge mistake? Or…

She didn't dare let herself hope.

Either she'd fidgeted so much that she'd woken Brad, or he was awake already and was waiting to hear the change in her breathing to tell him that she was awake, because he said softly, 'Good morning.'

'Um, good morning,' she said awkwardly, wriggling round to face him.

He stroked her face. 'Sunday morning. I do actually have food in the house, so I could make pancakes, if you like.'

It was the best thing he could've said to make her relax again, because she had a flashback to the only time he'd ever tried to make her pancakes, one Sunday morning back in their Cambridge days. She laughed. 'What, and set the smoke detector off?' He'd burned the pancakes so badly that the alarm had shrieked madly, and he hadn't been able to stop it. Although she'd finally managed to make it stop by flapping a damp tea towel beneath the smoke detector, the noise had woken everyone in their block of flats and she'd had to bake a massive batch of cookies to mollify their disgruntled neighbours.

He laughed back. 'Or maybe we could go out for breakfast. Though not in Great Crowmell—maybe somewhere a bit further down the coast.'

'Breakfast.' Where was he going with this? Was this some kind of date, or did he have something more serious in mind?

'We need to talk,' he said.

'You have a point.' At least if they were out somewhere, she could always leave and get a taxi home if things got too much for her. If they had breakfast next door, or even here, it could be awkward. Better to be somewhere that had an escape route. 'I'll meet you next door in twenty minutes.' Which would give her enough time to shower, wash her hair and change.

'Twenty minutes,' he said.

And the way he brushed his mouth against hers was so sweet it almost made her cry.

Fortunately nobody spotted her going from his cottage to hers. It wasn't exactly a walk of shame, but as she was still wearing her bridesmaid's dress it would be obvious that she hadn't slept in her own bed, and she'd hate someone to see her and gossip about her. Especially as she didn't have a clue right now where this thing between her and Brad was going. Was that kiss just now a goodbye or a hello? Was he going to say a final goodbye to her over breakfast? Was that what he'd meant by closure? Or did she dare hope that last night had meant something to him, just like it had meant something to her, and he'd ask her if they could maybe try again?

Could they make it work, this time?

Then again, today was the last full day on his lease of the cottage. Brad was due to go back to London tomorrow, and for all she knew he might have decided to return today. He'd been away from the lab for a week, and she knew he'd be itching to get back to his work.

She'd better not hope for too much. It would be naive, foolish—and, worse, it would be setting herself up to have her heart broken all over again.

Brad knocked on her door twenty minutes later. Like her, he was dressed casually in jeans and a T-shirt. 'Ready?'

No. Part of her was terrified. 'Sure,' she fibbed, and walked over to his car with him. He drove to a larger town a few miles down the coast, and they found a café that was part of a chain. As they sat down, Abigail felt almost too sick to eat.

As if he'd guessed, Brad said gently, 'You need to eat and so do I.'

She ordered coffee and an almond croissant; she could do with the sugar rush. Brad, as she could've predicted, chose a full English breakfast.

She crumbled half the pastry on her plate and forced herself to eat the other half.

And then she looked at him. 'So. Closure. I assume you're leaving either today, or tomorrow morning before eleven because that's when the cleaners come in to get the place ready for the next holidaymakers.'

He tipped his head on one side, an old gesture that made butterflies swoop in her stomach. 'I was planning to go back tomorrow. But it doesn't have to be that way.'

She frowned, not understanding. 'How do you mean?'

'You and me. We can't go back.'

So this *was* goodbye, then. 'Uh-huh.' She couldn't trust herself with actual words.

'We're different people now. Older. Wiser. And maybe if we'd met for the first time yesterday at the wedding, we might have…'

He actually blushed.

'Well, I wouldn't have been quite such a troglodyte with you,' he said. 'It's not my style. But I would have asked to see you again.'

He was still attracted to her. Just as she was still attracted to him.

'And if we'd met for the first time yesterday, I wouldn't have gone from the wedding reception straight to your bed,' she said.

'That's not your style, either,' he agreed.

'But if you'd asked me out…' Was that what he was trying to do now?

That meant this all hinged on her.

She could say no. Leave the past in the past.

But saying yes didn't mean that she was trying to recreate the past, either. She knew what he meant. If they'd just met for the first time, they'd maybe start dating. Take things slowly. See where things took them.

But that was the problem. They couldn't do that. Not when they lived more than a hundred miles apart. It wasn't a commutable distance, and she didn't want a weekend-only relationship. Particularly as she worked at least part of every weekend. 'Your life's in London,' she said.

'And yours is here. I know.' His dark, dark eyes were as irresistible as a puppy's. 'But let's ignore that for the moment. When you opened your new ice cream parlour, you didn't do the whole lot in a day, did you? Just as I don't expect a whole project to be sorted out in a day. Things take time. You need to do a critical path analysis before you start—work out what the steps are and in which order they have to be taken.'

She couldn't help widening her eyes at him. 'You're seeing us as a *project*?'

'No. I know it sounds as if I'm being a nerdy scientist, but I'm not.' He raked his hand through his hair. 'What I'm trying to say is that the obstacles you think are going to be a problem at the start of something don't always turn out to be obstacles. And, if the end result is important enough to you, then you can find ways to work around the obstacles.'

'Right.'

'So we could agree to put the issue of where we live to one side for now,' he said, 'and see where things take us. Starting with whether we actually like the person each of us has become.'

She coughed. 'I woke up in your bed this morning, Brad. I'd say that means we still like each other—at least physically.'

He smiled. 'The Abby I knew would've been too shy to say that.'

'I'm not shy any more. I'm comfortable in my own skin.'

'I'd noticed.'

Was that a criticism?

The question must've shown in her face, because he said, 'That was a compliment, Abby. Confidence is sexy.'

'Oh.' This time it was her turn to blush.

'So we've established that we're still attracted to each other,' he said. 'I have a lot of annual leave accrued. I could shock everyone in the lab and actually take some of it—and maybe we can spend some time together. See what else there is between us.'

Her frown deepened. 'You want to have a holiday here? With me? But I can't just take time off from work at short notice, Brad. That's not fair to my team.'

'I know, and you don't need to. I know the summer's your busiest time. It would just be nice to spend time with you—say, when you're free in the evenings or on your days off.'

'What I don't understand is, why now?' Why had he waited five years, if he'd still wanted her? Why had he even divorced her? She wasn't buying his knight on a white charger line.

'Because I had a few conversations at the wedding that made me think,' he said.

'Conversations?'

'With people who took a second chance at happiness,' he explained.

She couldn't remember anyone on the guest list who'd broken up and got back together. Her confusion must've been obvious, because he said, 'My mum, for starters.'

'You mean your mum and George?' She blinked. 'I saw him at the wedding yesterday. So your mum told you about him?'

'Yes. I don't expect her to spend the rest of her life alone,' he said. 'She's still relatively young. She should be enjoying life instead of being miserable and lonely and mourning Dad.'

Abigail really hadn't expected him to take the news so well. 'I'm glad you recognise that,' she said carefully.

He narrowed his eyes at her, as if to say that of course he did—that he'd grown up in the years since Jim's death.

'I assume you met him yesterday, then, and talked to him?'

Brad nodded. 'He seems like a nice guy, though I'd like the chance to get to know him better, to talk to him properly away from the hustle and bustle of the wedding.' He sighed and pushed his plate away. 'I want Mum to be happy. And Ruby.' He paused. 'And maybe you and me... Are you working today?'

'No. Lucy, my second in command, is in charge until tomorrow.'

'Then spend today with me, Abby.'

How could she resist those dark, dark eyes? 'What did you have in mind?'

'You. Me. A trip out.' He gave her a sudden grin, reminding her of the teenage boy she'd married, and her heart felt as if it had done a funny little flip. 'But we need to get you some travel-sickness tablets first.'

She suddenly realised what he was planning. 'You want me to go out on a boat?'

'Not piloted by me, but yes.'

'The Broads?' The medieval peat diggings that had turned into a waterway system over the centuries would hopefully be calm, like a millpond. As someone who'd grown up at the seaside, Abby knew she should've developed a decent pair of sea legs, but within five minutes of being on a boat she usually turned green. The swell of the ocean, even at its mildest, always made her queasy.

'I was thinking the North Sea,' he said. 'It's been a while.'

Five years. Unless he'd gone out on a boat some time this week, which she doubted—she rather thought he might have told her about it—she was pretty sure Brad hadn't been anywhere near a boat since Jim's death. So was this his idea of closure?

Then again, he'd just been talking about coming back for a few days. Spending more time with her.

It left her more confused than ever.

'What do you want, Brad?'

'Right now—a boat trip to see the seals at Blakeney Point,' he said.

She knew he'd avoided her real question, but she wasn't sure she was ready to hear the answer; she wasn't sure she could answer the question herself. Plus she liked the idea of the trip; it would be fun to go out and see the summer colony of common seals basking in the sunshine on the spit of sand, with their huge eyes and pretty faces. It had been years since she'd done it. 'OK, if we can get tickets.' It was a popular trip and weekends were usually heavily booked.

'I'll get tickets.'

He was so sure. And it was easier to go along with him, to buy bottled water and sea-sickness tablets and take the medicine to give it time to work.

He took her hand as they walked back to the car, and it felt weirdly like their early dates, when just the touch of his hand against hers made her feel as if fireworks were going off in the sky.

This was dangerous. Totally stupid, in fact. OK, so they'd spent last night together and she had no regrets about it whatsoever—but, even though Brad had told her to ignore the obstacles, she couldn't get away from the fact that his life was in London and hers was here. She wouldn't expect him to give his up for her, just as she wasn't prepared to give hers up for him.

Wouldn't it be better just to part now, as friends?

By the time she'd gathered her thoughts, he'd already driven them to Blakeney, they'd picked up their tickets and were walking across the marshes towards the harbour.

'Just for today,' he said, 'I think we should forget the past. We're not going to pretend it didn't happen—but we have to accept that we can't change it. All we can do is learn from it and move on. I know I hurt you and I'm sorry. I was too young to deal with what happened. Which honestly isn't an excuse, by the way, it's an explanation.'

She nodded. 'I understand. I was too young to deal with it, too.' And she needed to be fair about this. He wasn't the only one to blame. 'We both made mistakes. I hurt you, too.'

She'd left him when he was vulnerable and in pain and totally unable to deal with his feelings, when she should've tried harder to support him. 'I'm sorry.'

'Apology accepted.' He stopped and spun her round to face him, then kissed her.

His mouth was soft and so very sweet, and it sent a shiver of pure desire through her.

'Enough of the past. Today's all about you and me discovering a bit more about who each other is now,' he said. 'Let's have some fun.'

He climbed easily into the boat and helped her in beside him, then slid his arm protectively round her when they sat down. The captain took the boat out to the narrow strip of land at Blakeney Point, where everyone could see the seals basking on the sand. Some were lumbering along in an ungainly fashion; others were just sunning themselves. There were a few groups of a cow, a bull and a pup; Abigail knew that the pups on the land with their mothers were less than three weeks old, still needing to be fed.

Around the boat, seals were gliding through the water, looking far more elegant than they did on land and totally at ease; others were frolicking in the shallows, splashing their flippers in the water. It was utterly charming and Abigail lost herself in the moment, enjoying the sight.

'Smile for the camera,' Brad said, and took a snap of her on his phone with the seals in the background. She smiled at him and took a shot of him on her phone, too. Today was a good day. One to make memories.

'Would you like me to take your photograph together?' a middle-aged woman sitting near them asked.

'Thanks, that'd be lovely,' Brad said, and handed over his phone.

'Are you on honeymoon?' she asked as she took the photograph. 'You look like newlyweds.'

Abigail had no idea how to answer. The truth was much too complicated.

Brad simply smiled and said, 'Something like that. It's a lovely part of the world,' as if neither of them had ever been here before.

'Well, I wish you both every happiness,' the woman said, and handed his phone back.

'Thank you,' Brad said.

'Yes—thank you,' Abigail added with a smile.

Once they were back at the harbour, they climbed out of the boat and walked hand in hand back to his car.

'OK?' he asked.

'Yes. It was lovely. I'd forgotten how gorgeous the seal pups are,' she said. 'And those big eyes.' Dark and expressive and utterly captivating.

Though she could've been talking about Brad.

'Sea legs holding up?'

'They're pretty much propped up by the sickness tablets,' she admitted. 'But I'm OK. You?'

His hand tightened round hers. 'Good company and the perfect view. I'd forgotten how lovely the seals are, too.' He paused. 'Shall we go for a drive and find a pub somewhere for lunch?'

'Sounds good.'

Though Abigail couldn't shake what the woman had said about them looking like honeymooners.

This felt almost like a honeymoon. Not that theirs had been a conventional one: after Gretna Green, they'd done the coast-to-coast walk to raise money for the local lifeboat service and stayed in little guest houses along the way. They hadn't been able to afford an expensive holiday abroad when Brad was a student, though they'd pooled their birthday and Christmas money and managed a couple of nights in Paris. His dream of trekking through the Australian outback and hers of seeing the Northern Lights had been completely out of range of their budget. But they'd enjoyed snatched days out, visiting museums and booking train tickets well in advance to keep costs to a minimum.

There had been good times. Plenty of good times. It hadn't mattered that they didn't have much money. The only thing that had mattered was being together. Just like they were now; they didn't have to fill every moment with chattering. That hadn't changed over the years, and she was glad that they could still find an easy silence between them.

And it was easy for lunch out to stretch into pottering around antique shops in one of the Georgian market towns, and then afternoon tea, and then strolling along the beach and watching the stars come out.

Outside her front door, he said, 'I can't quite bear to let you go yet. Come and sit with me for a bit?'

But curling up together on the sofa led to kissing. Which led to him taking her back upstairs to the king-sized bed and making love with her; and then she was too comfortable to move.

'Stay with me tonight,' he said, wrapping his arms round her.

Common sense meant she ought to go. 'I have work tomorrow. And you've got to pack and be out of the cottage by eleven,' she pointed out.

'It won't take me long to pack,' he said. 'And I'll be leaving early. I have things to do in the lab.'

Back to the real world. Where no doubt Brad would think about this weekend and realise that this was all a pretty fantasy, but it couldn't work in real life. The logistics were impossible.

'But I'll be back. Give me a few days to sort things out,' he said. 'I need to make sure the project's still on track, and then I can call in a few favours and take a few days off.'

Maybe he would. Maybe he wouldn't. He'd been away for a week already; what if there had been some real developments on his project while he was away that meant he had to stay in London? What if he couldn't use his leave because some of his team had already booked holiday and that would mean the lab was short-staffed?

Her worries must've shown on her face because he kissed her gently. 'Stop overthinking things, Abby.'

'Habit,' she said.

'Tonight, let tomorrow take care of itself,' he said. 'Go to sleep.'

She didn't think she'd sleep, but eventually the warmth of his arms around her did the trick and she drifted off.

The next morning, he woke her with a tray of coffee and toast.

'Breakfast in bed?'

'Time to wake up. It's an hour and a half after sunrise,' he said with a grin.

'At this time of year, that means it's still really early,' she reminded him.

'Early enough for you to have time for your run before work.' He kissed her and climbed back into bed beside her. 'So. I'll leave by seven, which means I'll be back in London at around ten. I'll let you know as soon as I've sorted out some time off. I'll book a room in a hotel.'

'So you're not staying with your mum?'

'No. Though, this time, it isn't because I can't face the memories. Now I've been back to the house—and, thanks to you making me talk—I know I can. This time, it's about you and me,' he said, 'and we're keeping it simple. Staying at my mum's would mean that she'd ask too many questions.'

Abigail sipped her coffee. 'I guess the simplest thing would be to ask you to stay at my place.'

He shook his head. 'I wasn't fishing. And, actually, staying with you would complicate things.'

'How?'

'I think we both need our own space while we work out what's happening between us and what we want to do about it,' he said. 'I'm going to stay at Little Crowmell rather than here, if I can.'

Where the staff would be less likely to know him and less likely to be curious. 'OK. Well, let me know.'

'I will.'

When they'd finished breakfast, he kissed her goodbye. 'Thank you for giving me a second chance,' he said. 'I don't intend to let you down again.'

But there was a wide, wide gap between good intentions and what actually happened, she thought. They could start again. But what if they hit a rocky patch? Could she be sure that he wouldn't close himself off again?

'Uh-huh,' she said, not wanting to start a fight.

'I'll call you,' he said. 'Enjoy your run and have a nice day.'

'Safe travels,' she said. 'And I hope you don't get stuck in a traffic jam.'

'Thanks.'

When Abigail came back from her morning run, she saw that his car had gone.

And how ridiculous was it that she felt so flat?

She needed to prepare herself for the fact that Brad might get back to real life in London and change his mind. That in a few days she'd have a cool, apologetic text from him saying sorry, he'd realised that it wasn't going to work and it was best to keep things formal and polite between them.

But in the meantime she had work to do. A business to run. So she'd concentrate on that.

CHAPTER SEVEN

ABIGAIL THREW HERSELF into work to keep herself occupied and stop herself checking her phone constantly during the day. Brad didn't text to let her know he'd got back to London safely; then again, she thought, he was probably doing pretty much the same thing as she was. Plus he'd been away from the lab for longer than she'd been away from the café, even if he had been in touch with his team by phone. He'd be too busy to think about anything else but his job.

She finally picked up a text from him that evening, just as she finished locking the café behind her.

Hope you've had a good day. Can I video-call you later?

So was this it? Had he had time to think about it and change his mind? If so, at least he was going to tell her sort of face to face.

Sure. What time?

She didn't get an answer until she was back at her cottage.

Let me know when's a good time.

So the ball was in her court. I'm home now.

To her surprise, a few seconds later, her phone buzzed with a video call.

'Hey.'

She narrowed her eyes as she noticed the background. Unless Brad had turned his home into a lab... 'Are you still at work?'

'Um, yes,' he admitted.

'Brad, it's gone eight o'clock.'

'I know, I know. But I started late.' He smiled at her. 'How was your day?'

'Busy but good. Yours?'

'The same. I'm calling in a few favours, and I'm taking ten days off from next Monday evening.'

So he really meant it. He was actually coming back to Great Crowmell, to spend time with her and see whether they still had something between them. And she was shocked to realise how relieved that made her feel. 'OK,' she said, hoping that both her voice and expression were light and cheerful and didn't betray her feelings too much.

'I'd better let you get on,' he said.

Which was Brad-speak for *I'm busy but I don't want to be rude to you*, she remembered. 'Don't spend all night in the lab.'

To Abigail's surprise, Brad contacted her every day during the week; sometimes it was just a brief text, sometimes it was a phone call, and sometimes it was a video call. But every day she knew he was thinking about her, and that made her feel good.

On Thursday morning, a parcel arrived for her at the café. She opened it to discover a paperweight in the shape of an ice cream, together with a message in Brad's neat handwriting.

Just wanted you to know I'm thinking of you.

She knew he'd be busy in the lab, so she didn't want to disturb him with a phone call; instead she texted him a picture of the paperweight on her desk, so he could pick up the message at a time to suit him.

Thank you. It's brilliant. And very useful.

And what was sauce for the goose…

She wasn't set up to do mail order cakes, but she knew a good local supplier. And they'd just released a new flavour of sponge cake: sticky toffee pudding. Brad's all-time favourite dessert, unless that had changed—and somehow she didn't think it had. It took only a couple of minutes to order one to be delivered to him the next morning, together with a message.

Don't stay too late in the lab tonight.

Much later in the day, her phone pinged with a text in reply to her photograph.

My pleasure. Flowers would've been more conventional but would also have meant gossip, so I thought you'd prefer the paperweight.

He had a point.

And he actually called her in the middle of the day on Friday. 'I just got your delivery. Thank you. Is this the next step in your empire?'

Abigail laughed. 'No. But it's a local firm and Ruby's office uses them,' she said, 'so I've tried four different varieties. I nearly sent the apple crumble one—it's gorgeous with lots of cinnamon—but then I saw the sticky toffee pudding and I was pretty sure you'd like it.'

'It's fabulous. My team says to thank you, too.'

'My pleasure. Don't work too late.'

'Yeah, yeah.' But she could hear the laughter in his voice. 'Speak to you soon.'

And did she actually hear him mutter 'love you', just before he disconnected the call, or was that just what she'd wanted to hear so her ears were playing tricks on her?

She didn't have the courage to ask him. But there was definitely an easy affection between them again. A warmth that hadn't been there for a long time—a warmth she'd missed. She liked the man he'd become, and she rather hoped he liked who she'd become, too.

Abigail was run off her feet over the weekend, and was pretty sure that Brad was just as busy in his lab; but then on Monday evening, when she left the café, she picked up a text from him.

Leaving now.

The message was timed an hour ago, so he was already on the way.

Staying at the Bay Tree Hotel in Little Crowmell.

The hotel was attached to a golf course and had a spa; her stomach tightened for a second as she remembered the last time she and Brad had stayed in a hotel with a spa. The weekend away she'd won in a competition. The weekend when everything had gone wrong, and their life together had unravelled faster than she'd ever believed could happen.

She shook herself. Five years. Older and wiser, she reminded herself. They were different people now, and these were different circumstances.

Meet me in the bar for a drink at about nine?

Just the two of them. The start of something that might or might not work out.

But that was the whole point of this time together. To see what they might still have—and whether it was worth the possible upheaval. Because, if they were to have a future together, they'd have to find some kind of compromise about where they lived.

See you at nine, she texted back. She knew he wouldn't get the message while he was driving, but he'd maybe pick it up if he stopped for a break, or when he got to the hotel.

She changed into a pretty top and smart black trousers, and called a taxi to take her to the hotel for nine; it meant she could have a glass of wine with Brad without worrying about being over the limit for driving home. And how strange that she felt like a teenager about to go on her first date with a boy she'd secretly liked for months. Second time round, shouldn't it all be calm and collected and adult? But she could hardly wait to see him. Just like the years when they really had been teenagers, sneaking time together between their studies.

There was a group of businessmen in the bar, all wearing lanyards; clearly they'd been at some sort of conference in the hotel and were letting off some steam after a hard day's work, judging by the amount of hearty laughter and empty glasses at their table. There was no sign of Brad. Maybe he was still in his room.

Abigail went over to the reception desk. 'Excuse me, please. I'm meant to be meeting Bradley Powell here. I wondered if you could call his room for me, please?'

The receptionist checked her computer. 'Sorry, he hasn't checked in yet.'

He'd probably been held up in traffic, Abigail thought. 'When he does check in, could you let him know that Abigail Scott is waiting for him in the bar, please?'

'Of course,' the receptionist said with a smile.

Feeling slightly awkward, Abigail ordered an orange juice at the bar, and tried to find herself a quiet corner. She was playing a word game on her phone to keep herself busy while she waited, when one of the businessmen came over to her, holding an almost empty pint glass.

'On your own, sweetheart?' he asked.

'No, I'm waiting for someone,' she said.

'Well, you can have a drink with me while you're waiting.'

He sounded slightly drunk, slurring his words, and Abigail sighed inwardly. She was used to dealing with difficult customers over the years, so she knew how to keep the situation from escalating. She kept her voice calm and anodyne. 'It's very kind of you to offer, but no, thank you.'

'But a girl as pretty as you *needs* company.'

She forbore from correcting him that she was a woman, not a girl, and suppressed her irritation. It looked as if she was going to have to take the cracked record approach. 'It's very kind of you to offer, but no, thank you,' she repeated firmly.

'Go on, sweetheart. What's the harm in it?' He swayed towards her.

'No, thank you,' she said yet again.

'It's only a little drink, sweetheart. Come and join me and the boys. We could do wi—'

'I said no, thank you,' she cut in. 'Now, would you please leave me alone?'

'You don't mean that, sweetheart.' He looked her up and down. 'Or maybe just you and me, then, not the boys.'

Abigail had had enough. She stood up and was at the point of walking over to the bartender and asking him to deal with the man when Brad walked over to her.

'Sorry I'm late, darling. Reception told me you were waiting in here for me.' He greeted her with a kiss. 'Traffic was horrible and my phone decided not to work, so I couldn't call you and warn you how late I'd be, and...' He looked at the man who'd been trying to chat her up, and suddenly seemed to be six inches taller and broader. 'I'm sorry, I don't believe we've met,' he said politely, though his voice contained a hint of steel. 'Are you a friend of my wife's, or maybe one of her business associates?'

'I... Sorry.' The man raised his free hand in surrender and backed away as if he'd been scalded. 'No offence, darlin'. I didn't know. I didn't mean anything.' And, to Abigail's relief, he stumbled off back to his colleagues.

'Wife?' Abigail asked quietly, raising her eyebrows.

Brad smiled. 'I forgot to add two letters and a hyphen.' Then his expression became more serious. 'It looked as if the guy was pestering you.'

'He was. I was about to go and talk to the bartender and ask for help,' she admitted.

'It might still be worth having a word with the reception desk, so they're aware of the situation and can make sure he doesn't behave like that to anyone else,' he said. 'Though obviously that's your call.'

She liked the fact that Brad wasn't bossing her around. 'I will. Have you checked in?'

'Just about. And, actually, I did text you to say I was stuck in traffic and I'd be late.'

'I didn't get your message.'

'I'm sorry.' He paused. 'Have you eaten tonight?'

She nodded. 'Have you?'

'I grabbed a burger from the place on the corner, on my way out of the lab. It's fine. Can I get you another...?' He looked at her glass. 'That looks like orange juice, so I'm assuming you drove here.'

'Actually, I got a taxi so I could have a glass of wine or something with you.'

He smiled. 'That's good. Let me order a bottle of wine, and maybe we can go and drink it on the terrace.' He looked at her. 'Or I believe my room has a balcony, if you want to go somewhere quieter. And, just so you know, that offer doesn't come with any strings attached.'

The bar was becoming noisy and she really wanted to get away from the group of businessmen. Their over-hearty laughter was starting to irritate her. 'Actually, your balcony would be nice.'

'OK. What would you like me to order?'

'Dry white, please. Or red, if you'd prefer,' she added swiftly, not sure what he drank nowadays. 'I really don't mind.'

'Dry white's fine with me.'

Part of Abigail felt sad that they still had to be polite to each other. There was a time when Brad would've known what she'd like without having to ask, just as she would've known what he wanted.

'I'll talk to the hotel reception about that guy while you sort out the wine,' she said.

The receptionist was horrified and apologetic. 'I'll ask the duty manager to have a quiet word with him and make sure the bar staff don't serve him any more alcohol this evening,' she said.

'Thank you,' Abigail said. 'I'm fine, but anyone younger or less able to deal with the situation might have struggled, and I'd hate someone vulnerable to be in that position.'

She'd just finished talking to the receptionist when Brad came to join her, carrying a bottle of Sauvignon Blanc and two glasses. 'All OK?' he asked.

'Everything's fine,' she confirmed.

They went up to his room, and she noticed that he hadn't even unpacked; clearly he'd just dumped his suitcase on his bed and come immediately to find her.

He opened the French doors to the balcony, which overlooked the golf course on the top of the cliffs, and the sea glittered in the distance. There were two wrought-iron chairs, a small wrought-iron table just big enough for a couple of drinks, and one of the hotel's trademark bay trees in a terracotta pot.

'Very nice,' she said.

'Indeed.' He gestured to her to sit down, and poured them both a glass of wine. 'I'm sorry I was late. There was a traffic jam.'

'It isn't your fault that the text didn't come through.'

'But I'm still sorry. If I'd been on time, you wouldn't have been bothered by that guy.'

She reached over to squeeze his hand. 'I'm not blaming you. And it's fine. No harm done.' She smiled at him. 'So you've got ten days, you said?'

'I did,' he confirmed. 'Sunetra—my assistant manager—is keeping all the projects ticking over. I can review things through my laptop here during the day, and she'll call me if there's anything she needs.'

Abigail would be busy herself during the day, so his work wouldn't intrude on their time together. 'That's good.' She looked at him. 'So does your family know you're here?'

'Ruby's on honeymoon. She doesn't need to know. But, yes, I told Mum,' he admitted. 'She's promised not to interfere. What about you—did you tell your mum and dad?'

'They kind of noticed that we left Ruby's wedding at the same time,' she said. 'So, yes, they asked me about you.' And her mum was worried about it; she'd seen how long it had taken Abigail to pick herself back off the floor and dust herself down after the divorce.

'They don't approve, do they?' Brad asked wryly.

'They have some reservations,' she said. 'But they won't interfere. This is between you and me. Our chance to work out if we like who each other is now and if we want to do something about it.' She paused. 'So what's the plan?'

'Plan?'

'You were the one who talked about running a project. About critical path analysis.'

He smiled. 'I'd hardly call you a project,

Abby. But the plan, as you put it, is to spend time with you. If we were dating under normal circumstances, we'd see each other, what, once or twice a week?'

'About that,' she agreed.

'Then think of this as a kind of speed-dating. If we see each other every day for the next ten days, it's the equivalent of nearly two months of dating at once or twice a week. And then we'll have a better grasp of the situation.'

'We'll know whether we want to take this thing further or not.' And, if they did, then they'd have to decide which of them would be the one to uproot their life.

'We could make a list,' he said. 'Things we want to do, places we want to go. Make it as off-the-wall or as touristy as you like.'

She looked at him with a smile. 'Spoken like a true scientist.'

'Isn't that what you do in business?' he asked. 'Make lists and plan things?'

'I have a list of new flavours I'm planning to try, and promotional activity, yes,' she admitted.

'So let's start here. I don't mind being scribe—I'll copy the file and send it to you when we're done, and then we can whittle it down.' He took his phone out of his pocket and flicked into what was obviously a note-taking app.

'Let's do the obvious ones,' she suggested. 'A walk on the beach, a visit to the gardens of a stately home, a walk in the woods.'

He typed them in. 'A trip on one of the steam trains—I'm fairly sure there was a nineteen-forties weekend listed in the local newspaper. That could be fun.'

'OK. Visit a ruined castle, go somewhere quirky for afternoon tea.'

'Agreed. And we need stuff for rainy days. I know it's summer and this is the driest part of the country, but this is England and that means rain. Museums, art exhibition, ten-pin bowling.' He typed them in swiftly.

'The cinema,' she said. 'Maybe going to see a local band.'

'And the lighthouse,' he said. 'I haven't been there for years. We need to make that on a day when it's open to the public and we can climb up to the lamp.' He smiled. 'There are so many things on that list I've never done before. I guess you always take where you live for granted.'

Not just where you live, she thought. It was too easy to take people for granted, too. Maybe that had been part of the problem between them, the first time round. She'd been so sure she knew how he'd react in any situation—and how very wrong she'd been.

'Well. To us and our list,' she said, lifting her glass. 'And may it give us our answers.'

'I'll drink to that,' he said, lifting his own glass. 'So when are your days off? Then we can plan to do the further away things on those days.' He narrowed his eyes at her. 'You're smiling.'

'You really are making this into a project, aren't you?'

'It just makes sense to do it this way and make the most of our time.'

'Like you did when we went to Paris.'

'You remember Paris?' His voice was suddenly husky.

She nodded. 'You had a list of all the places we wanted to visit, the opening days and times, whether they were covered by our museum card, and you even marked everything on a map.'

'But we got to see everything,' he pointed out. 'The Mona Lisa, Notre Dame, the Eiffel Tower, Montmartre, and all the Monets.'

'True. Though it would've been nice just to go for a wander in the city and see what we could find.'

'But we only had three days. If we'd been wandering around aimlessly, we would've missed all the other stuff we actually wanted to see,' he reminded her.

How different their approaches were: Brad with his strict itineraries, and her own preference for just seeing what they came across. Maybe they were too different now for things to work between them. Nowadays, she would've insisted on one of those three days in Paris being spontaneous. On closing their eyes and putting a finger at random on a map, and using that as their starting point for exploring. But was that too far out of Brad's comfort zone?

'Do you remember, we bought all those postcards at the art galleries and museum and stuck them on our living room wall, because we couldn't afford a proper print in a frame?' he asked.

'I remember. And that guy did a charcoal drawing of us at Montmartre,' she said, 'when we were both sitting on that wall outside the church.'

'What happened to that?'

She spread her hands. 'No idea.' The drawing had been another casualty of their broken marriage.

As if Brad realised they were heading into dangerous territory, he backtracked. 'So, when are your days off?'

She made a show of checking her diary, even though she knew her schedule without having to look it up. 'This week, I have a full day off on Thursday, and a half-day on Sunday. Next week, I have a day off on Monday; I need to go in on Wednesday first thing, but I'll be done by ten.'

And then on the Thursday he'd go back to London.

When it would be decision time.

Would they make it together as a couple— or would they agree to part for good and ignore the pull of the past?

Right at that moment she had no idea.

Brad made a note. 'I'll work through our list and make—'

'—an itinerary,' she finished.

'You say that as if it's a bad thing.'

'No. Just sometimes it's good to be spontaneous.'

'I can do spontaneous.' And he proved it by putting his phone down, coming over to her side of the table, scooping her out of her chair and then sitting in her place and settling her on his lap.

And of course she had to put her arms round his neck for balance.

She could hardly complain, given that she'd

been the one to make a fuss about him being so buttoned-up and such a planner.

'I thought you said your balcony didn't come with strings?' she asked.

He stole a kiss. 'It doesn't. I'm not expecting you to sleep with me, and I'm not asking you to stay the night with me. Even though we're sort of speed-dating for the next few days, I'm not going to rush you.' He stole another kiss. 'But it's good to hold you again, Abby.'

She stroked his face. 'It feels good to have you hold me, too.'

'I'm glad that's settled.'

And then there was no need to talk. They just sat there together, warm and comfortable and snuggled up, watching the afterglow of the sunset and the stars shining more brightly in the sky as the night darkened.

Finally, he kissed her again. 'You've got work tomorrow. And I meant what I said about no strings and not expecting you to stay the night.'

'It'd just confuse things. We're meant to be seeing how it goes, what we still have left between us,' she agreed. 'I'll call a taxi.'

'But if you want to come for breakfast tomorrow, just show up,' he said.

'Maybe.' She slid off his lap and called the taxi. 'They'll be ten minutes.'

'OK. And thank you for giving me a second chance.'

'I think we're giving each other a second chance,' she corrected.

But had they both learned enough from the past? Would they make the same mistakes all over again? Was this going to be the best idea they'd ever had or a complete disaster?

CHAPTER EIGHT

ON TUESDAY, ABIGAIL took her usual early-morning run to see the sun rise over the harbour, and thought about whether to turn up at the Bay Tree for breakfast with Brad.

Then again, today was supposed to be their second date. And she had a pile of work to do. In the end, she sent Brad a brief text.

Up to eyes this morning. See you tonight. A x

He responded with an email she picked up at her desk.

See you tonight. Let me know what time. Itinerary attached. B x

She opened the file, read it and smiled. The whole way he'd organised it was so very Brad. A table, with the date in the left-hand column, and suggestions for what they did, split between fine weather and wet weather, and with notes of opening times for the places they'd wanted to visit.

Tonight's itinerary was a walk on the beach after work—unless it was raining, in which case they'd go to the cinema or ten-pin bowling. He'd even noted which films were showing during the week, so she could choose what she liked.

He'd already crossed out the gory ones—so he obviously remembered that horror films gave her nightmares, even if they were award-winning and brilliantly written. But there was a comedy and a sci-fi film listed that she thought they might both enjoy, so she marked them as possibles.

She texted him.

Thanks for itinerary. See you at seven.

Then, on impulse, she added, Can't wait.

Can't wait to see you either, came the reply.

It warmed her all day and, although Abigail had intended to experiment with a new flavour of ice cream that morning, she ended up messing up the recipe twice because she was thinking of Brad and couldn't concentrate. And she found herself clock-watching when she was doing admin during the first half of the afternoon—until she noticed that it was raining. The kind of deceptively fine rain that would soak you to the skin and make any beach walk completely miserable; and she knew that the café would start to get really busy with holidaymakers who were fed up with the rain and wanted a hot drink to warm them up. Now wasn't the time to daydream about her beach walk with Brad, which she was pretty sure would have to be postponed. She wasn't a ditzy teenager any more. She had a business to run and staff to support.

She went into the café and helped out behind the counter until the rush had died down; and, when even the diehard dog-walkers had left and the café was practically empty fifteen minutes before they were due to close, she sent everyone home early.

'But don't you want us to clear up before we go?' Joe asked.

'It's fine, sweetie. I'll sort it out. We're practically empty now and you were all rushed off your feet earlier.' She patted his shoulder. 'Off you go.'

Once the last customers had finished their drinks and left and she'd cleared up, locked the door, and stacked the chairs, she was just about to wipe down the tables and mop the floor when there was a knock on the door.

Frowning, she went over to explain that sorry, the café was closed now until tomorrow—only to see Brad standing there. Much earlier than they'd agreed.

She let him in. 'Hey. I wasn't expecting to see you, yet.'

'I thought maybe you could do with a hand.'

She hadn't expected that, either. 'Are you just bored waiting for me?'

He laughed. 'A tiny bit. But my plan was, if I help you clear up, you'll be finished more quickly and then you can come and play with me.'

'Spoken like a true scientist. Do you want to do the floor or the tables?'

'Whichever you don't want to do.'

She handed him the mop and bucket.

'So do you clear up on your own every night?' he asked.

'No, but after the rain caught out some customers, it drove the rest away so I sent everyone home early.'

He looked at her. 'Now I get why your staff are so protective of you. You're good with them.'

'They stay late without being asked if we've got a rush on,' she said, 'so it's only fair to let them go earlier if we're not busy.'

'And the fact that you're prepared to do

every single job in the café, including mopping floors and cleaning toilets.'

'Are you telling me you don't help your team scrub the glassware if you've been really busy in the lab?' she asked.

'Of course I do. We're a team.'

'Exactly my point,' she said. 'I might have got the job originally because I'm the boss's daughter, but I worked my way up from the ground floor. And I don't expect my staff to do anything I haven't either done myself or am prepared to do.'

'You didn't get the job because you're the boss's daughter,' he said. 'You worked your way up in Cambridge. You already knew how to run a team and how to organise your stock. You got the job because you earned it.'

She *had* earned it. She'd thrown herself into work, put in crazy hours, to stop herself thinking of Brad after they'd split up.

And now they were dating again. Ten days of speed-dating to see if there was still something between them and if they could make a go of things second time round.

Did she need her head examined? Was this going to be a huge mistake? Had they both changed enough for this to work, or had they changed so much that they'd be even further apart?

Suddenly flustered, she said, 'Well, this café isn't going to clean itself,' and busied herself cleaning tables. Between them they finished cleaning the café so it was ready for the morning; and while they were working the rain grew heavier.

'I think our beach walk might've been rained off,' he said ruefully as rain lashed against the plate-glass windows.

'Just a tad,' she said with a smile. 'Thanks for helping.'

'No problem.' He tipped his head on one side, and her heart felt as if it had done a little flip. 'Cinema or ten-pin bowling?'

'Toss a coin?' she suggested.

'Heads, cinema; tails, bowling. That OK with you?' At her nod, he took a coin from his pocket and tossed it. 'Ten-pin bowling it is. Where are you parked?'

'Outside my house,' she said. 'I walk in when the weather's good—which it was, this morning.'

'That makes things easier. I'm parked right outside,' he said.

She locked up, and they walked hand in hand to his car.

'So I guess this is our first official date?' she asked, once they were sitting in his car.

'It is. Which means I have to be gentlemanly and let you win at bowling.'

She loved the way his eyes crinkled at the corners and scoffed. 'Bring it on.'

'So you're telling me you don't need the bumper bars up at the sides any more when you play?' he teased.

'I'll have you know zig-zagging the ball is a perfectly valid form of bowling,' she said.

He laughed. 'In your dreams.'

He drove them to the out-of-town complex which housed the bowling alley, cinema and half a dozen restaurants. 'Actually, I haven't done this for quite a while,' he said.

'Getting your excuses in early for when you lose?' she teased.

'Just saying.' He smiled. 'Have you already eaten, or shall we grab something to eat first?'

'Dinner sounds good,' she said. 'So I'll buy dinner and you can pay for the bowling.'

'Strictly speaking,' he said, 'the dating was my idea so it all ought to be my bill.'

'Strictly speaking,' she countered, 'we made that list together, so we're going halves. No arguments. So I'm buying dinner and you're paying for the bowling, and I might let you buy me a beer at the bowling alley if you're good.'

* * *

Brad really liked the woman Abby had become. Funny, smart and confident. In the old days, she would've simply gone along with his suggestions. Now, she had the confidence to say what she wanted. 'OK. Halves, it is.'

They went to one of the fast-food places and ordered a sharing platter of grilled chicken, sweet potato wedges, garlic bread and avocado salad. And every time his fingers accidentally touched hers as they reached for garlic bread or sweet potato wedges at the same time, every nerve-end in his body tingled. Anyone would think he was seventeen again, not twenty-seven. Though at least nowadays he was more articulate than he'd been as a nerdy teen.

'Thank you for dinner,' he said when she insisted on picking up the bill.

'My pleasure.'

And funny how her smile made his heart feel as if it had done a somersault. It was anatomically impossible; but she was the only woman who'd ever made him feel that way.

He enjoyed the bowling, too. He was so aware of Abigail and the graceful way she moved, even though she was still absolutely terrible at ten-pin bowling.

After the first game he ended up putting

up the bumper bars for her. 'At least this way we can both have some fun. There's nothing duller than seeing your ball go in the ditch every single time,' he said.

'You just want to admire my zig-zag skills,' she said, brazening it out.

He laughed and stole a kiss. 'You bet.'

They'd had so much fun as teens. And as a young married couple, even though money was tight, with him as a student and her with a low-paid job. They'd just revelled in being together.

Tonight had reminded him very much of how much he'd appreciated her company. Why had he ever been so stupid as to let her go?

The more time he spent with her, the more he wanted to be with her. This week was his opportunity to convince her to give him a second chance. He needed to work harder at this than at anything else he'd ever done in his life.

At the end of the evening, he drove her home and parked in the nearest space he could find to her front door.

Crunch time.

Had he done enough for her to let him see her again tomorrow? There was only one way to find out. And he was shocked by how nervous he felt. This was worse than sitting his driving test, his finals, and his viva for his doctorate all rolled into one. And the outcome also felt more important.

'Was tonight's date OK enough for you to meet me tomorrow?' he asked, trying to keep his tone light.

'Ten dates. That's what we agreed,' she said.

Whether she'd enjoyed tonight as much as he had or not, she was at least going to be fair about it. Give him a chance to prove himself. 'OK. So tomorrow evening's a walk on the beach,' he said. 'Or, if it's raining, this time we can maybe do the cinema.'

'That sounds good.' She leaned over and kissed him, and it sent a shiver of pure desire through him. 'Thank you. I had fun, tonight.'

'Me, too.' And, because he didn't want to push her too far, too fast, and ruin any progress he might have made, he didn't ask if he could come in for coffee. He simply brushed his mouth against hers really lightly, not deepening the kiss the way he really wanted to. He knew they were still compatible in bed, but that wasn't what this was about. It went much, much deeper than that. 'Goodnight, Abby. See you tomorrow.'

He waited until he'd seen her close the front door behind her, then drove back to the hotel.

* * *

On Wednesday evening, it was dry, and the café was still incredibly busy when Brad got there.

He could offer to help clear up again; but that would leave her open to gossip. He was pretty sure a couple of her staff recognised him, and the last thing he wanted was for them to start asking awkward questions. He'd left his car in the town, so he couldn't sit there and wait until she was ready. In the end, he bought a cold drink and sat at a quiet corner table until one of her staff—one who didn't know him—said, 'I'm ever so sorry, sir, but we're closed now.'

'And you need to put the tables and chairs inside. Of course.' Brad stood up.

'Thank you.' The young man smiled at him. 'Have a nice evening.'

'Thanks.' Brad smiled back, and went to sit on the dunes. Abby clearly wasn't going to finish dead on seven tonight, so he texted her to make sure she didn't feel pressured.

Sitting on dunes right now. Didn't want to get in the way of your staff. Come and find me when you're ready.

It was another twenty minutes before Abigail emerged. 'Hey. Sorry I'm late.'

'Not a problem.' He stood up, and, as he'd hoped, she kissed him hello.

'Had a good day?' she asked.

'Yes. Sunetra sent me a file to review, so that took a while. And I had lunch with Mum.'

'Who was dying to know the latest?'

'Yes, but I'm giving her credit—she didn't ask.'

'She's waiting until you're ready to tell her.' Abigail smiled. 'That's one of the things I like about your mum. You know she's concerned and she's there, but she's not pushy.'

'No she's not.' He took her hand. 'How was your day?'

'It's always busy when it's sunny. Which is how I like it.' She slipped her hand into his. 'Where did you park?'

'In town. I assumed you walked here this morning, as it was dry, and I thought I could walk you home from here.'

'That's nice.'

And it *was* nice, walking hand in hand on the beach. The tide was starting to come in, but not massively fast, so he knew they still had time to wander along the shoreline for a bit.

Out of sheer habit, he glanced down at the sand. As usual, there was a scattering of razor shells, cockle shells and limpets; but in between he spotted a pretty banded shell and stooped to pick it up. 'For you,' he said, and handed it to Abigail.

She inspected it. 'That's a nice one. It'll go well in the dish of shells on my bathroom windowsill. Thank you.'

'Do you remember, we always used to look for stones that look like letters?' he asked. 'After you saw that picture of a stone alphabet on the Internet.'

'We found an S, once and what could almost have been a Y,' she said. 'But we never did manage to find an A, a B and an X, did we?'

'Though we did find a heart-shaped stone.' He still had it, tucked away in a drawer somewhere, a memory of much happier times. 'Do you still look for letter-shaped stones?'

She shook her head. 'Not since you.'

'Shall we?'

She looked at him, and there was the ghost of sadness in her eyes. But then she nodded, and they continued walking hand in hand along the beach. It didn't matter that they weren't chattering; the silence was companionable rather than awkward. Eventually, she tugged at his hand, then bent down to pick something up from the sand.

'Not a heart-shape or a letter,' she said, 'but still interesting.'

The stone had a perfect hole bored right through the centre.

'A hag stone,' she said. 'Legend has it that you can see through the hole into fairyland and it can protect you against bad luck. It's meant to be lucky to hang it from a ribbon.'

'Superstition,' he said. 'It's actually a composite stone where the softer part's been worn through by water.'

'Sometimes it's more fun to forget the science and enjoy the old stories,' she said.

'You don't have to forget the science,' he said. 'You can see a sun dog in the sky and know it's caused by the refraction of sunlight off tiny ice crystals—but knowing how it works doesn't mean you can't still appreciate the beauty of the phenomenon.'

'Brad?' she asked.

'Yes?'

'Shut up.' And, just to hammer her point home, she kissed him.

His head was spinning by the time she broke the kiss. She clearly knew it, because she grinned. 'I'm glad that still works.'

He couldn't help laughing. 'OK. I was being pompous.'

'Just a little bit. But at least you know it.' She handed him the stone. 'Thread it on a ribbon,' she said.

'I will.' And he meant it. 'Let's head back into town. Have you eaten since lunch?'

'No,' she admitted. 'I've been too busy.'

'Fish and chips or pizza?'

'Pizza,' she said. 'We could eat at my place.'

'I'd like that,' he said.

They picked up a takeaway pizza from the pizzeria in town, then headed back to Abigail's cottage.

'So how is it, being back again?' she asked.

'As a tourist? Fine.'

'Why did you stay away for so long?' she asked. 'I mean, I can understand it'd be hard for the first year, with the first birthday, Father's Day and Christmas to get through.' And the mess of their divorce. So many memories to stop him in his tracks. 'But why did you never come home after that, even for Christmas or your mum's birthday?

'I always see Mum for her birthday and Christmas,' he protested. 'And I see Ruby. I video-call Mum at least twice a week.'

'Which isn't the same thing as coming home.'

He blew out a breath. 'I know. Since you ask, I just couldn't face it. There were too many memories, too much unfinished business that will never get closure now.'

'Unfinished business?' She didn't understand. Like her, Brad and Ruby had had an idyllic childhood, growing up with parents who adored them. They'd all been popular at school and done well academically; Brad had won every single science prize. She couldn't think of anything that would count as unfinished business. Unless... 'Do you mean *us*?'

He shook his head. 'Not that. It doesn't matter.'

She thought it did, but he had that closed-off expression in his eyes that she knew only too well. Time to back off. Maybe if she gave him time to think about it, he might open up and help her understand what was in his head—and she could help him deal with it.

'But yes, before you ask, I feel guilty about not coming back. I know I was selfish. But I can't change the past, Abby.'

'No.' But you could learn from it. 'Was it as bad as you thought it would be?'

'No,' he admitted. 'I think, the longer I left it, the more it built up in my head and the worse I felt. It was easier to use work as an excuse to avoid coming here. But I'll make more effort in the future.'

She hoped so—for his mum's sake. 'OK. I think you're talked out for now. Are you up for something different for pudding?'

He looked relieved that she wasn't pushing him any further. 'Bring it on.'

'Correct answer,' she said, and took a tub from the freezer.

'New recipe?'

'Very, very old one, more like,' she said. She served him a scoop, then sat with her elbows propped on the table and her chin resting on her hands, watching him.

'Aren't you having any?'

'Maybe later. I want to see your reaction,' she said.

'Are you turning into a scientist, now?' he asked.

She laughed, liking his sense of humour. 'No. I just want to see your face when you try it.'

'I'm not even going to ask,' he said, and tasted a spoonful.

She saw the exact moment he realised what he was eating. And that it wasn't actually sweet.

'That,' he said, 'is really not what I was expecting.'

'Is that you being polite and you don't like it?'

'No. Now I've adjusted my mindset, it's quite nice.'

'Normally I'd serve this with slices of fresh apple or pear,' she said. 'Or really good crackers. But I wanted you to try this on its own, first.'

'For the shock value.'

She laughed. 'Busted.'

He took another spoonful. 'So is this what sparked off your idea for dog ice cream?'

'Yes—after I tried it at the Old Boat House, I looked up some old recipes and gave it a go. Mum brought Waffle over and I dropped some on the floor—and you know what dachshunds are like. He scoffed the lot. And that was my lightbulb moment.' She smiled. 'But I use cheddar for the dogs rather than Parmesan.'

'I still can't quite believe I'm eating cheese ice cream.' He took another spoonful. 'It's good.'

'Thank you. I haven't actually got any crackers in at the moment, but I can slice you an apple if you like.'

'It's fine just as it is,' he said with a smile. 'When you were talking about my reaction, I did wonder if you were going to give me the dog ice cream.'

'I could,' she said. 'I only use human-food-grade ingredients—partly because the owners don't believe it at first and want to taste it themselves. But I have an official panel of canine testers, including Waffle, Ollie the

Collie—' his mum's dog '—and the dogs of all my staff.'

'So you have regular doggy tasting evenings?'

'Give me a sec.' She flicked into the photo albums on her phone, found the picture she was looking for, and handed him her phone. 'Here we go.'

He chuckled. 'I love it. Doggy testers all in a row, with their owners holding the tubs for them to lick. And is that a chocolate flake?'

'No, it's a mini dog biscuit,' she said.

'You ought to send this to the local press,' he said.

'I got there before you. It's their photograph,' she said. 'My suggestion, and they loved it.'

'You're amazing. I always knew you were creative, but this is something else,' he said. 'Your mum and dad must be so proud of you.'

'I like to think I'm taking the family business forward. In a couple of slightly different directions, admittedly—but it's all customer-driven.' But it really warmed Abigail that Brad thought her parents should be proud of her. That he recognised the hard work she'd put in to Scott's in the years since they'd split up. That she'd changed and grown.

'You're amazing,' he said again.

He insisted on washing up; but he accepted her offer to stay for a while. And it was nice, just being curled up on the sofa together with his arms wrapped round her and soft music playing in the background.

Maybe she should ask him to stay.

But the whole idea of these two weeks was speed-dating—ignoring their past and looking towards their future. In terms of that, they were two dates in: the equivalent of a week in a relationship. So asking him to stay the night would be too soon.

As if he was thinking the same thing, he shifted so that he was sitting properly on the sofa again. 'I ought to go.' He leaned over and kissed her lightly. 'So I'll see you tomorrow at ten.'

'And we'll climb the lighthouse.'

'It won't matter if it's raining because we'll still have amazing views. And I thought we could have a picnic somewhere afterwards, maybe go inland and find a nice shady forest if it's really hot. Or sit in the car if it tips down.'

Typical Brad: he planned all outcomes. 'Sounds good. What would you like me to bring?' she asked.

'Nothing—the picnic's all mine. And yes, I know I probably ought to buy it from

Scott's, but...' He wrinkled his nose. 'Then it wouldn't be a surprise.'

She laughed. 'I'm not that territorial.'

'Good.' He stole a kiss. 'Is there anything you'd rather I didn't get?'

'I'm fine with whatever you'd like to pick,' she said with a smile. 'Surprise me.'

'I think you win on the surprise front with the Parmesan ice cream,' he said wryly, and kissed her goodnight. 'Sleep well.'

On Thursday, Brad knocked on Abigail's front door at ten; as he'd expected, she was ready. She never had been the sort who took hours to get ready.

They headed further down the coast until the red and white striped lighthouse came into view.

'Can you imagine what it'd be like, living in a lighthouse?' she asked. 'This one's actually on the mainland so it wouldn't have been so bad. But it must've been so tough, years ago, if you were the keeper of an offshore lighthouse. No telephone, no mail, no visitors—just you and the lighthouse and the other keepers for months, and no fresh food because there wouldn't be space to grow any.'

'You'd have a boat coming to bring your mail and supplies once a week, and you could go fishing when you weren't on duty in the lighthouse,' he pointed out.

'Yes, but you'd have hardly any fresh vegetables and fruit, except on the couple of days after the supply ship came, and think of the sheer isolation.' She shuddered.

'But think of the views—all the stars you'd see.' He looked at her, remembering one of her big bucket list items. 'Maybe even the Northern Lights.'

'If you were in one of the lighthouses in Northumbria or Scotland, perhaps,' she said.

'And the birds you'd see. It would be great if you were an artist—Ruby would love it.'

Abigail laughed. 'Your twin likes being smack in the middle of modern life. She'd enjoy the sketching for maybe a week, and then the isolation would drive her crackers. And imagine her with no phone coverage.'

'True,' he admitted.

'I think it'd be too isolated for me,' she said. 'Though I guess for you it'd be like being in your lab.'

He smiled. 'I'm not that isolated in my lab. Apart from the fact that I work as a team, I have to go to way too many meetings during the week.'

He parked the car and they walked down the track to the lighthouse; it turned out they were among the first to queue for the tour and were let up with the first batch of holidaymakers.

'It's barer than I expected,' Abigail whispered when they were inside. 'Obviously this bit must've been for storage because the lighthouse keeper had a cottage next door.'

There were colourful displays around the walls, with old photographs of the lighthouse and former lighthouse keepers, but when Brad looked up there was nothing between them and the very top floor of the lighthouse.

Their group followed the guide up the narrow stone steps that clung to the walls in a spiral, first of all up to a room full of maps, which showed all the shipping hazards in the area and the locations of other lighthouses nearby.

'When the lighthouse was first built here, it took three keepers to run. And they had to be really good friends because they worked together and lived together for months at a time. It wasn't so bad here on the mainland, but in somewhere like the Needles Rock on the Isle of Wight it meant living in a tiny room, with no running water or heating.'

Brad looked at Abigail, who grimaced at the thought of it.

Then they climbed up the steep ladder to

the lamp itself; from the top, there were amazing views over the cornfields and the sea.

Brad was fascinated by the fact that the light was only five hundred watts but was visible eighteen miles out to sea, thanks to the angles of the glass slats around the lamp. But, as the guide talked, he thought about how much his dad would've loved this, and a wave of sheer misery and loss hit him. It felt like a wall slamming into him and he was barely able to pay attention to what the guide was telling them about how the lamps worked in the early days and what the keepers had to do, from lighting and checking the lights to keeping records of the weather and any shipwrecks.

Abigail frowned. Brad had gone very quiet and it was as if all the sunlight had been sucked from his face.

Something was definitely wrong. Was this something to do with his 'unfinished business'?

Would he talk to her about it? Or would he block her off again?

She had to concentrate on going backwards down the steep ladder from the top, and going down the spiral steps was definitely more scary than going up them, but as they walked to the car she took his hand and squeezed it. 'Are you OK?'

'Sure.'

But his tone was flat. Years ago, she would've left it. Now, she called him on it. 'You don't look OK or sound OK.'

He sighed. 'I was thinking about Dad. He would've loved this, all the stuff about boats in olden times. I could've brought him here and taken him out for a pub lunch or something afterwards.'

'I know. It's a shame you never got to do it.' She turned to face him and splayed her hand over his heart. 'But your memories of him are still right here and you'll never lose them—and you can still share this with him in your head.' She added quietly, 'And today you've shared it with me.'

'I know. Sorry. I'm not good company right now.' He grimaced. 'Do you want me to take you home?'

At least he was talking to her. 'No, let's go for a walk somewhere. It will clear your head.'

He was quiet all the way as they drove inland to a patch of woodland. He was quiet, too, when they walked hand in hand through the trees, and she didn't push him to talk.

Eventually, he sighed. 'I'm sorry. I don't

want to bring you down with my mood, but I don't want to shut you out either.'

Relief flooded through her. He wasn't going to close himself off again. 'It's fine,' she said lightly. 'Everyone has good and bad days.'

'Do you get bad days?'

She had when they'd first split up; she'd managed to pull herself out of it, but it had taken her a while. And she'd really needed the support of her parents and her best friend—support she guessed Brad either hadn't had or, more likely, had refused. Support she should have given him instead of letting him down. 'Yes. Obviously both my parents are still here, so it's not the same thing that you went through, but I'm only human. I get days where just about everything seems to be wrong.'

'So what do you do? How do you deal with it?'

'Hit my kitchen,' she said. 'Baking always works for me. I think it's the scent of vanilla that does it. Actually, I read an article saying it's not just childhood associations with the scent that cheers people up—there's something in the fragrance that's calming and reduces stress, the same way as lavender works to help you sleep and lemon's good for if you're feeling sick or need to be mentally sharp. And that's proper peer-reviewed science, not the woo-woo stuff,' she added with a grin.

He smiled. 'You sound a bit like me.'

'It's where I got it from,' she said with a smile. 'I kind of picked up from you what to look out for and what to ignore. But, seriously, do you want to skip the picnic and go back to my place for a baking session and see if it works for you?'

He raised an eyebrow. 'Have you forgotten the time I made you pancakes and we couldn't shut the smoke alarm off?'

She laughed. 'No, but I'll be supervising, and I promise it's the easiest recipe ever. It's also the best management tool ever.'

'Management tool?' He looked mystified.

She grinned. 'I make them for my staff—they love me and will say yes to almost anything once they've scoffed the brownies.'

'Got you.' He nodded. 'OK. I'll give it a go. But it'd be a shame to waste the picnic.'

'Let's eat first, then.'

They headed back to the car, where he retrieved the cool bag containing their lunch, before finding an empty table at the picnic area.

Brad had chosen a wonderful selection of food: sourdough bread, Brie, tomatoes, ham carved off the bone, local crab and chilli pâté, local raspberries and smoothies from the local deli.

'This is fantastic. Excellent choices,' she said.

'Glad you like it,' he said.

On the way back to the car, they saw magpies. Three of them.

'One for sorrow, two for joy, three for a girl,' Brad said, recalling the old rhyme.

'Maybe Ruby will have a honeymoon baby,' Abigail said lightly.

She and Brad hadn't discussed children when they'd got married; their tacit agreement was that they wouldn't even discuss it until he'd finished his studies. By then, they'd been divorced, so it wasn't an issue. Now, it might be. She'd barely dated since Brad, let alone met someone she'd think about settling down with and having a family with, and she was pretty sure it was the same for him.

But now they were on the verge of trying again…

They looked at each other, and she knew both of them were thinking the same thing, wondering if the other wanted children.

It was a conversation they might need to have—but not yet. Not until they'd decided what was happening between them.

'Let's go make some killer brownies,' she said.

She could see in his face that he knew she'd chickened out of the conversation—but that he was relieved she hadn't made an issue of it.

Back at her house, she took the ingredients from her cupboard.

'Do you always have ingredients for brownies?' Brad asked.

'These ones, I do.'

And it was so simple: weighing the dry ingredients into a bowl, measuring the wet ones into a jug, and stirring the lot together with a whisk.

'See? It's not so very different from lab work,' she said.

'Oh, but it is,' he said with a smile.

But as the scent of the brownies spilled from the oven, she could see his mood change. He relaxed enough to make them both a mug of coffee—and funny how nice it felt to have him pottering around her tiny kitchen.

He kissed her when she'd taken the brownies out of the oven. 'Thank you. You're right. The scent of vanilla and chocolate *has* made me feel better.'

'Of course I'm right. I have two X chromosomes.' She gave him a cheeky grin.

He didn't correct her; he just smiled and kissed her again.

'Now go and take these to your mum, then take her out to dinner. You can return the pan later,' she said.

'Are you sure?'

'I have stuff to do,' she said, 'and I think you need some time with your family right now.'

'Yeah.' He held her close. 'You're wonderful, do you know that?'

'I'm just me.'

But it warmed her all the way through when, an hour later, her doorbell went and the local florist handed her the most beautiful arrangement of flowers.

The card was in Brad's handwriting and said simply, *Because you make my world a better place.*

Abigail had to blink back the tears. Today had been a little bit of a hurdle, but they'd overcome it. So maybe, just maybe, there was hope for the future.

CHAPTER NINE

BRAD CALLED FOR Abigail at seven on Friday evening and she greeted him with a kiss. 'Thank you for the flowers. I know I texted you, but it's good to say thank you in person, too. They're gorgeous.'

'You're welcome.' He looked slightly awkward. 'Sorry I was a bit difficult yesterday.'

'It's fine. You talked to me.' And that was the big difference between now and five years ago, she thought. The thing that gave her hope for the future. There was still stuff he was keeping inside, but she'd give him space and let him talk when he was ready.

'Mum says thanks for the brownies.' He handed her the now clean cake tin.

Abigail smiled. 'She's already texted me to say thanks.'

His eyes widened. 'Did she ask…?'

'Of course she did. She's your mum and she worries about you. But I told her,' Abigail said softly, 'that we're talking, that right now we're not in a place to make any decisions, but she'll be among the first to know when we do.' She stroked his face. 'And she's not going to rush us. When we make the decision, it has to be right. For both of us.'

'Agreed.' He kissed her. 'Come on. Let's go and play.'

He'd got tickets for them to see a singer-songwriter in a tiny venue in Norwich, where the bar was lit by fairy lights and the stage was just about big enough for three people, two guitars and a piano. It reminded her of their years in Cambridge when they'd go to see a band in some tiny room and stand at the front, with his arms wrapped round her, swaying along to the music and enjoying the closeness as well as the atmosphere.

They couldn't go back to the past.

But maybe they could move forward and bring the best bits of the past with them.

On Saturday night, they went to the cinema, and Brad even put up with a rom-com and held her hand all the way through it. He got his steam train trip on Sunday afternoon, and their seats were in an old-fashioned carriage with seats opposite each other and a corridor, with a uniformed inspector coming to clip their tickets. And Abigail had to admit it was fun, with the sulphurous smell of coal in the air and the sight of the steam wafting past the windows as they went round a bend in the track.

Monday felt like a honeymoon: a day to themselves in Norwich, where they went to an art exhibition in the castle and wandered through narrow streets full of quirky, independent shops. They had afternoon tea in a café where all the china was clearly vintage and none of the tables and chairs matched, but she loved the ambience: ancient pine dressers where jars of local honey and home-made jam were stacked for sale, the paintings on the walls were all by local artists and were for sale, and they had a kitsch cuckoo clock which gave the café its name. The scones were light and fluffy, the sandwiches were perfect and the red velvet cake was the best she'd ever tasted.

On Tuesday, Brad picked her up after work and they had a fabulous dinner on the terrace at his hotel before sitting on his balcony with a bottle of champagne, watching the sun set.

Two more days, she thought, and their speed-dating thing would be over. It would be time to make their decision about the future.

Dating him over the last few days had

shown her that yes, she was still physically attracted to him and still enjoyed his company. Spending time together was fun.

And if she was honest with herself, she knew she was still in love with him. In love with the man he'd become rather than the memory of the teenager she'd married. Brad was thoughtful, kind, and he made her laugh. If he asked her to stay with him, she knew she would.

But how did he feel about her?

He'd sent her those flowers. He'd opened up to her—at least, he'd tried to. He'd said that she made his world a better place; that was how she felt about him, too.

So if he did feel the same way that she did… What then? How was it going to work, given that her life was here and his was in London? It wasn't a commutable distance. How were they going to compromise?

'You're quiet,' he said, his arms wrapped round her and his mouth against her hair.

'Wool-gathering,' she said, not wanting to push the point.

'I was thinking,' he said. 'I know you have to be up early tomorrow, but right now I don't want you to go home.'

Her stomach suddenly felt as if it were filled with butterflies. 'You're asking me to stay the night?'

'Yes.' He twisted slightly so he was facing her, and snatched a kiss. 'I know we said we weren't going to complicate things, but I want to wake up with you in my arms.'

She wanted that, too.

'And I'll drive you back to your place tomorrow morning at whatever time you like.'

'It'll be really early. Well before breakfast,' she warned.

'I don't care, as long as you stay,' he said.

In speed-dating terms, they were practically two months in to their new relationship. And although she knew they'd both held off sleeping together again because they hadn't wanted sex to get in the way, she was already clear about what she wanted. The fact that he wanted it, too—and he'd talked about waking with her, not about sex—gave her hope.

And how could she resist those beautiful dark eyes? She took a deep breath. 'Yes.'

'Good.' He kissed her, scooped her up at the same time as he got out of the chair they'd been sitting in together, and carried her to his bed.

Abigail was awake early the next morning. Brad was still asleep and the light was just starting to filter through the curtains. He really was beautiful, she thought as she watched him lying beside her. But more than that, she loved the man he'd become.

They'd find their compromise somehow. Even if it meant that she was the one who had to uproot her life and move to London. Maybe she could open a branch of Scott's there, while putting a manager in to run the Norfolk side of the business.

She'd miss her parents, Ruby, her friends and her colleagues. She'd miss seeing the sea every day. She'd miss the tiny flint cottage she'd grown to love. Leaving here would be a massive wrench.

But it meant she would be with Brad.

No more loneliness, no more wishing that she'd done something different and managed to save her marriage.

Tomorrow, they'd talk about it and make their decision.

And please let him want the same thing that she did.

She woke him with a kiss. 'Hey, sleepy-head.'

He was almost instantly awake. 'I need to drive you home.'

'I can get a taxi.'

'I promised you last night I'd take you home, no matter how ridiculously early it is.' He kissed her. 'Good morning. I can try sweet-talking the kitchen staff into letting us having some very early breakfast.'

She smiled. 'It's fine. I'll grab something after I've had my shower and changed.'

In the end, he drove her home and made her coffee while she showered and dressed, and instead of her usual morning run she made toast and had breakfast with him.

And how nice it was to do something as simple and everyday as having breakfast together. She'd missed that. Missed him making her coffee, missed doing the crossword together on Sunday mornings, missed waking up in his arms.

'I'm afraid I have to go now, but I'll be done at the café by ten,' she said.

'Sure. I'll do the washing up while you're gone.'

'It's fine. Leave it. A couple of crumb-filled plates and jammy knives really don't matter,' she said, flapping a dismissive hand. 'But thanks for the offer.'

She let him drop her at the café on his way back to the Bay Tree.

'I'll pick you up at the café at ten?' he asked.

'See you then,' she said, kissing him goodbye.

She could hardly wait to see him again.

And she loved the gardens of the house he'd discovered that only opened to the public four times a year; it was full of specimen trees, and early summer was the perfect time to show it off. They wandered through the gardens hand in hand, and Abigail gasped when they went down to the lake and saw the hundreds of azaleas there reflected in the water.

'I've never seen anything like this in my life. Our mums would both love it here.' She took a photograph.

'And with that bridge over the lake—it's stunning.' He squeezed her hand. 'I always meant to take you to Giverny to see Monet's gardens. I know you love that picture of the bridge and the lily pond.'

'And all the tulips in his spring garden,' she said. 'I'd love to see that.'

'I had so many plans for us,' he said. 'I wanted to make all your dreams come true.'

'All I wanted was to be with you.' And maybe it was time she took a risk and told him how she really felt about what had happened. 'I loved you, Brad. I thought you loved me. I had a few doubts when you asked me to elope, but I was so sure you loved me as much as I loved you. And then, when I realised you didn't, it was too late.'

'I loved you,' he said. 'But I admit I asked you to elope for the wrong reasons.'

It felt as if he'd slapped her, and her recoil was involuntary. As were the tears she had to blink away fast.

Clearly he'd noticed, because he said, 'That came out wrong. I meant every word of my wedding vows. I just...' He blew out a breath. 'I've never really talked about this to anyone, but Dad and I had a bit of a strained relationship.'

'What? But your dad adored you.'

'He wanted me to follow in his footsteps,' Brad said. 'Our fights weren't in public. But it was all the little comments he made. He never once criticised Ruby about her choice of career—I guess he could see that she lived for her art and that she was really good at it—but he didn't think much of my choice. "You'll never make a proper living. Lab technicians are ten a penny." He said that to me so many times.'

'You're not a technician. You're a researcher,' she said. 'Actually, I think you would have made a good lawyer, because you pay attention to detail and you pride yourself on doing a job properly—but your heart wouldn't have been in it. You did the right thing, choosing the subject you love.'

He looked at her. 'That's not how Dad saw it.'

And then she realised why Brad had really stayed away. Why he'd reacted so very badly to his father's death. *This* was the unfinished business. 'And you never got your chance to show him that you'd made the right choice because he died while you were still a student.'

Brad said nothing, but she saw the muscle clench in his cheek.

'Your dad,' she said, 'loved you very much. And if he'd wanted you to read law—well, yes, of course he'd be disappointed that you didn't. But, as I've said to you before, your dad was stubborn and wouldn't listen to anyone. It would have choked him to say, "Brad, you did the right thing." Even if you won the Nobel prize for chemistry, and you made the biggest scientific discovery of the century, he would probably still say that he was proud of you but you should have been a lawyer.'

Brad looked at her as if the whole weight of the world were on his shoulders.

'And then at his chambers he would have been telling everyone within earshot—and that would include the set of chambers three buildings away—how his clever son was a brilliant chemist and he was going to change the world.'

'You really think so?'

'I've got no reason to lie to you, Brad. He loved you and he was proud of you. Telling you to your face would have meant admitting he was wrong about your career choice, and that isn't what your dad did. But ask your mum. Ask Ruby. I bet they'll tell you the same thing.'

He sighed. 'I just wish I'd had the chance to show him I did the right thing for me.'

She hugged him. 'I reckon he knows. He's watching you right now, huffing about how his boy's gone soft in the head and of course he loves you. But then he'd add there was still time for you to do another degree and maybe specialise in science law.'

Brad was shaking.

Oh, dear God. She'd just sent him into another meltdown. 'Brad, it's OK,' she said, desperately wanting to reassure him.

But when he pulled back, she could see that he was laughing.

'What?' she asked, puzzled.

'What you just said... That's exactly what he would have said.'

'So I'm right about the rest of it, too.'

'I guess.'

'I loved your dad. I thought he might be a bit of a nightmare to live with—so full-on hearty, the whole time, it must have been a bit wearing—but I never realised he gave you such a hard time about your studies. I wish you'd told me. I could've…' She sighed. 'Maybe not.'

'Made it better? I think I needed to grow up and see it for myself,' he said. 'Which, thanks to you, I have, and I'm sorry I didn't trust you enough to tell you years ago.'

'Is that why you asked me to elope? So you'd be living with me instead of having to come back here and be nagged about your degree?'

He shook his head. 'It was a fit of rebellion. We had a big fight, that night. And it wasn't just the usual stuff about my career; he started on about you. He said we were too young even to be engaged. And I wanted to prove him wrong.'

She bit her lip. 'So you didn't actually want to marry me.'

'I always wanted to marry you,' he said. 'Dad was wrong about some of it—I never met anyone who even began to match up to how I felt about you—but he was right about us being too young to get married. I still had a lot of growing up to do. The fact I pushed you into eloping instead of having a wedding like Ruby's was proof of that.'

'I really thought you loved me. And when your solicitor sent me that letter…' Her throat felt as if it had closed up.

'More proof that I needed to grow up,' he said. 'I really loved you, Abby. But I was a mess and I really thought setting you free to find happiness with someone else was the right thing to do.'

'I never wanted anyone else.' She swallowed hard. 'I think you broke me for a while. I cried so much I couldn't see, my eyes were so swollen. And you wouldn't even speak to me.'

He held her close. 'I'm so sorry I hurt you. I'm not going to ask you to forgive me, because I can't ask for that. But I've learnt a lot about myself over the last few weeks and I know I'd react differently in the future.'

The future. The thing they were meant to be discussing tomorrow.

Did they *have* a future?

'I felt as if I wasn't enough for you,' she said. 'And it made me wary of dating again. In case whoever I started seeing felt like that about me—that I wasn't enough.'

'Any man who had you in his life would count himself the luckiest man in the world.'

'You didn't,' she pointed out.

'Because I was young, I was hurting, and

I was very, *very* stupid.' He stroked her hair. 'I can't change the past, Abby. I wish I could. And, if I could, I would never...'

'...have married me?' she finished.

'Have let you go,' he corrected.

'So are you saying you want to try again?'

'I'm saying,' he said carefully, 'we might both need a bit more time to think. We've told each other things we maybe weren't expecting to hear.'

She certainly hadn't had a clue about what he'd told her.

'We need to make the right decision for both of us,' he said, 'for the right reasons. And at this precise moment I feel as if someone's just put me on one of those loop-the-loop rollercoasters at triple speed.'

'So you want to go back to the Bay Tree on your own?'

'No. I want to walk through this garden with you, hand in hand,' he said.

Now she got it. 'And not talk.'

'Not talk for a little while,' he agreed. 'But I want to be with you.'

Walking in the sheer beauty of the gardens helped to clear her head. Maybe his, too, because finally he tightened his fingers round hers. 'I'm sorry.' He grimaced. 'I seem to be saying that a lot, today.'

'Maybe we need to put it all behind us,' she said. 'We can't change the past,' she said. 'But know that not all of it was bad.'

'Agreed.' He looked at her. 'Right now, I really want to kiss you. But it kind of feels— I don't know. Insensitive. And I'm trying to be sensitive.'

'You might be thinking too much,' she said.

'How?'

'This,' she said, and reached up to kiss him. 'That's better.'

He wrapped his arms around her and kissed her back. 'You're right. Much better. So here's the plan. I take you somewhere nice for dinner, we watch the stars come out over the sea—and then, if I'm not being too pushy, I want to fall asleep with you in my arms.'

'That,' she said, 'sounds like an excellent plan.'

CHAPTER TEN

BRAD STAYED WITH Abigail at the cottage that night, and it was good to wake in his arms. To wake and make love—except, when she got out of the shower, she realised that she was going to be late for work.

'I know I'm the boss, so technically speaking I can walk in any time I choose, but I need to set an example,' she said. 'I don't want anyone to think I'm slacking off.'

'Nobody thinks you're slacking off. I'll drive you in,' he said.

In the end, she was only ten minutes late, though it was enough to fill her with guilt.

He kissed her lightly. 'Go. I need to get back to the hotel, pack and check out. I'll see you at seven and I'll book a table somewhere tonight for dinner.'

'See you at seven,' she echoed.

But when Abigail walked into the café and smelled the bacon grilling, the scent made her feel queasy.

Maybe it was something she'd eaten at dinner last night. Something that hadn't agreed with her.

When her usual mid-morning mug of coffee made her stomach turn as well, to the point where she couldn't even take a mouthful of the stuff, she started to wonder. Was she being paranoid, or was she…?

She did a quick mental calculation and realised that her period was late. It should have started a week ago.

Panic skittered through her. Had they even used a condom, that first night—the night of Ruby's wedding? They'd definitely used protection since then, but that first time… Her mind was horrifyingly blank on the subject. She'd been so swept away by Brad that she couldn't think straight. She simply couldn't remember.

Could she really be pregnant? The dates would tie in. Friends who'd had a baby had talked about a super-enhanced sense of smell in the very early days of pregnancy and feeling sick, being tired, going off coffee, and their breasts feeling tender. And every one of those symptoms applied to her right now. She'd felt sick at the smell of cooking bacon, she didn't want coffee, and her bra felt too tight…

She pushed the thought away. How utterly ridiculous. The nausea could be anything, and not fancying coffee could be down to that too; she was tired because she was still putting in all the hours at work and seeing Brad every night; the tightness of her bra was purely psychosomatic because now she was half convinced that she was pregnant; and the date of her period was probably a bit off kilter because her emotions had been turned upside down over the last couple of weeks. The dates had nothing to do with it. Of course she wasn't pregnant.

But the thought kept nagging at her, along with the fact they'd seen those magpies in the woods the other day. *Three for a girl, four for a boy...* For pity's sake, it was just an old superstition. She wasn't pregnant.

By mid-morning, Abigail had had enough. There was only one way to find out the truth.

It was her admin day in the office at the café, so if she went out for a bit it wouldn't cause any problems with the staff at the counter. She made an excuse that she needed to go and see a supplier, and walked back to her cottage to pick up the car. She could've gone to the pharmacy in town or even the supermarket, but everyone knew her in Great Crowmell and she didn't want even the faintest bit of gossip to start. Instead, she drove to a supermarket in one of the bigger market towns where nobody knew her and bought a pregnancy test kit. A digital one, so there would be no margin of error.

She didn't want to wait and do the test at her cottage, so she went into the nearest café and ordered a cheese scone and a mug of hot chocolate.

She was probably being ridiculous. Of course she wasn't pregnant by her ex. She couldn't be. Though the test felt as if it were burning a hole in her bag.

How pathetic was that? She was twenty-seven, not seventeen.

But what if she was pregnant? What if? What if? The question ran round and round in her head.

She gritted her teeth, forced herself to eat the scone and drink the hot chocolate, then headed for the bathroom.

Thankfully it was empty and there were three cubicles, so she didn't feel guilty about causing any kind of queue. She did the test and stared at the little white stick.

One blue line, to show it was working...

And there it was. In stark black text, so she couldn't pretend she'd make a mistake and misread the result.

Pregnant.

She swallowed hard.

What was she going to do now?

Last time she and Brad had done something reckless—eloping to Gretna Green—they'd kept their castle in the air going for a few years… And then it had all come crashing down and she'd realised how naive and foolish they'd been.

Nearly ten years later, they hadn't learned a thing, had they? They'd been reckless and stupid, and had a crazy affair. Something that both of them had known deep down could never last. Abigail didn't expect Brad to give up his job for her—and, even though the other day she'd thought that maybe she could follow him to London, now it came down to it she wasn't so sure that she could. Her life was here. Her family was here. In London, she'd be isolated.

Or would Brad offer to give up the job she knew he loved and come back to Great Crowmell? Would he consider taking a job that maybe he didn't love so much? Would he want to make a life here with her?

And then the doubts came slamming in. What if he didn't? What if Brad did expect her to give up everything for him and move to London? What if she put a manager into the café and ran the business from a distance, so she wasn't letting her parents down—would things really work out between them? Because, the last time they'd been together and life had thrown up a major change, their marriage had disintegrated. Brad hadn't coped with the shock of his father's death and he'd frozen her out.

What if he did the same if things went wrong this time round?

OK, so she'd had the confidence to push him when he'd gone quiet on her at the lighthouse, and he'd opened up to her. But that was over something relatively small. What about something bigger? What if—God forbid—something happened to his mum, or to Ruby? What if he was made redundant and it was difficult to find another job? Would he talk to her and let her help her through it, or would he shut himself off again?

And a baby would be a huge, huge change to both their lives. They hadn't discussed having children; she had no idea how he felt. Was it too soon for him? Or didn't he want children at all?

Plus she knew that a baby was never the answer to a sticky patch in a relationship. Those early days, with all the broken nights and worry and stress, would put extra strain on them and would widen any rifts between them, to the point where those rifts couldn't be bridged any more. What if the baby made him feel trapped? What if he froze her out again? Because this time it wouldn't just be her, it would be the baby as well.

But could she do this on her own? Could she have a baby and keep running her family's business as a single mum?

There was another option, but she pushed it away. She'd made a choice that had led to a pregnancy, and getting rid of a baby just because it wasn't convenient felt wrong. Not that she'd ever judge anyone else for making that decision, but for her that wasn't the right option.

OK. She knew her parents would stand by her. So would Ruby, and Brad's mum. They'd all be supportive. But Brad himself...

She had absolutely no idea how he was going to react. Or how she was going to tell him. The only thing she knew was that they had to talk about it. Tonight. And only then could they decide if they wanted to move on together—or apart.

And until then she just had to keep going. Pretend that everything was just fine and she'd had a business meeting.

She splashed water on her face, then drove

back to the café and buried herself in all the admin tasks she hadn't done that morning. And please, please, let her find the right words to tell Brad.

The Abby Brad had dropped off at the café that morning had been laughing and bubbly, a little flustered and cross with herself, but happy.

The Abby he met at seven was quiet. Too quiet.

'Is everything all right?' he asked.

'Of course. Why wouldn't it be?'

But he'd seen a flicker of panic in her eyes. Which were grey, not green, another tell-tale sign that she was upset.

'Abby. Talk to me. Tell me what's wrong.'

'There's nothing wrong.' Her tone was light, but he could tell it was deliberately so; and it increased his conviction that something had happened.

He waited until they were seated at the quiet table he'd booked in a pub and had ordered their meal before tackling her again. Maybe something had happened to the business. 'Something's wrong,' he said gently. 'I'm guessing it's work. What's happened? Someone's gone bust, owing you a lot of money and you need a temporary loan to keep on track?'

When she said nothing, he pushed on. 'Because I've got savings, Abby, and they're yours if you need them. I've seen how you've grown your parents' business and you're a good manager, so I know you'll get through this. I'm more than happy to invest in Scott's if you need me to.'

'It's not that.'

To his horror, a tear slid down her cheek, followed by another. And then the tears were unstoppable.

He knew she'd hate it if the waiter came over and saw her crying like this. And he also knew something was really, really wrong. She needed him, and she needed them both to get out of here. Now.

'Go out to the car. I'll deal with everything here and then I'll be with you,' he said, handing her his car keys.

He went to see the waiter. 'I'm really sorry, but something's cropped up and we can't wait for the meal we've ordered. Can I pay the bill? And if I could have a bottle of water to take away, that'd be great.'

The waiter was nice about it, but it felt as if it was taking for ever to sort everything out; and Brad was totally at a loss as to what had upset Abby so much. If it wasn't the business, was it her parents? He knew she was close to them. Had one of them had bad news about their health? She'd said something about her mother being diagnosed with coeliac disease. Had that been masking something more sinister?

He was really worried by the time he got back to the car.

She'd stopped crying, but her face was pale and she was still looking worried sick.

'I don't have tissues,' he said, 'but I have this.' He handed her the bottle of water. 'I'm going to drive us somewhere quiet, then you're going to talk to me. I know something's wrong. If I can do anything to help you fix it, I will, but even if I can't then talking about it will help you feel a bit better.'

She looked at him. 'That has to be the most hypocritical thing you've ever said.'

He stared at her. 'What?' He couldn't believe she was picking a fight with him, when he was trying his best to be supportive.

'"Talking about it will help."' She actually used her fingers to make fake quotation marks round the words, and that stung. 'It didn't, five years ago.'

That stung even more, because he knew it was true—and because now she knew why.

'You mean, because I didn't talk,' he said. 'I've kind of learned that one the hard way.' He couldn't stop a note of acid creeping into his voice when he added, 'And, believe it or not, I might have grown up a bit since then.'

But Abigail wasn't one to pick a fight. She was straight-talking, but she didn't deliberately start arguments. 'You're trying to deflect me,' he said. 'Don't. Just tell me whatever it is.'

She lifted her chin. 'You're not going to like this.'

'Let me be the judge of that.'

She took a deep breath. 'OK. You wanted it straight, so I'll give it to you straight. I'm pregnant.'

As the words sank in, his head spun.

Abigail was going to have a baby.

His baby.

'But... How?'

'Oh, come on, Dr Powell,' she scoffed. 'You did biology A level and a doctorate in biochemistry—at Cambridge, no less. You *know* how babies are made.'

'Of course I know how babies are made,' he said. 'But how—?' No, that was the wrong question. 'When?'

She swallowed hard. 'It has to be the night of Ruby's wedding.' Her breath hitched. 'I can't remember if we used a condom. My head's blank. But it has to be then.'

He knew she was right. They hadn't made love again until two nights ago, and it would be way too soon for her to know that she was pregnant from then.

Had they used a condom, that first night?

He thought about it, and his head drew a blank, too.

And he didn't know what to say.

He opened his mouth, and nothing came out.

Panic flooded through him.

A father.

Would he even make a good father? Everyone had thought he was close to his own father, and in some ways he had been; but half the time he'd worked so hard, driven himself, just to prove himself to Jim. It had felt almost like being in a competition. And not in a good way.

He hadn't been great as a son, as a brother, as a husband. So how could he possibly be a good dad?

Abby knew that look.

She'd seen it in Brad's eyes before, after Jim's death. The look that told her he was bottling up his feelings and he was going to withdraw from everyone.

So much for thinking that they'd gone a long way to sort out the issues between them. So much for thinking that Brad would change. He might *want* to change, but maybe at the end of the day that was simply asking too much of him and he couldn't.

It looked as if she was going to be bringing up the baby alone.

No. No, no, no. Brad fought against the panic. This was where it had gone wrong last time, because he hadn't talked. This was way too important for him to mess up. Even if the wrong words came out, he could fix that. He might have to grovel for weeks, but at least they'd be talking. Silence was what would drive her away.

'Right now,' he said, 'I don't know what to say. I need to think about this. But what I do know is that I'm here for you. Now and always. That's not going to change. Ever.'

She didn't look as if she believed him. Then again, he'd let her down before. How did he convince her that it would be different, now? He took her hand. 'When did you first realise?'

'Today. When you dropped me off at the

café, I walked in and the smell of cooking bacon made me feel really queasy. And then I didn't want my coffee.' She dragged in a breath. 'I thought I was being ridiculous and making two plus two make twenty, until I counted back and realised my period's a week overdue.'

'So Ruby's wedding was right in the middle of your cycle.' He knew he was analysing this instead of making the right emotional noises, but for pity's sake he was a *scientist*. Analysing things was the way he managed his life. It was the way he'd work out what to do next. 'And you did a test?'

Another tear slid down her cheek. 'I even went two towns away to buy one, to a supermarket where I knew nobody would have a clue who I was.'

So nobody would gossip. That was the thing about living in a small town: everyone knew everyone else, and also knew all their business. If anyone had seen Abby buying a pregnancy test today, the whole of Great Crowmell would have known by now.

'Good idea,' he said. 'And it was positive.' It was a statement, not a question. Even though she was probably panicking every second that she waited for the results, Abby wouldn't have misread it.

She nodded. 'I bought one of the digital ones, the ones that actually use words instead of coloured lines, so there could be no mistake. No squinting at it and trying to work out if there's really a line or if you just think it's there. Plain text.'

'Also a good idea,' he said.

She was pregnant.

With his baby.

If this had happened when they'd still been married, he would've been thrilled. He would still have been a student, so money would've been tight, but they would've managed.

Now, financially he was in a much better position. He'd inherited money from his father and invested it well; plus he'd been promoted rapidly at work. If Abigail wanted to stay at home with the baby, he could afford to support her.

Emotionally, they could still be poles apart. These last few days, he'd thought they'd grown closer. He'd known that he was still in love with the woman who'd stolen his heart when they'd been teenagers. He'd woken up with her in his arms this morning, and he'd felt happier than he had in years. Tonight was supposed to be about their future. About whether they were going to give each other a second chance and get back together.

Technically, she'd be the one giving him a second chance. He was the one who'd messed up.

But now the situation was different. She was expecting their baby. So there was only one thing they could do, and everything else would just have to fall into place from that. 'OK. It's obvious what we have to do. We'll get married again,' he said.

CHAPTER ELEVEN

THAT WAS BRAD'S answer to their situation? A blithe 'we'll get married again'? No discussion, no finding out how she felt, no telling her how he felt? Abigail could barely believe what she was hearing. And this couldn't have been further from the first time he'd asked her to marry him, when he'd promised to love her for the rest of time.

'No,' she said.

He frowned. 'What do you mean, no?'

'We haven't discussed *anything*, Brad. Not how we feel about each other, not whether we actually want to keep seeing each other in the future, not the logistics with me living here and you living three hours away in London...' She shook her head. 'We can't get married.'

'It's not as simple as just whether we want to see each other or not,' he said. 'The situation's changed. We have a baby to consider now.'

'And that's why I can't marry you,' she

said. 'Last time we were married, your dad died and you didn't cope with it. You pushed me away—and I let you do it, so it's not all your fault and I'm not dumping the blame on you. But you froze me out, Brad. Next time we have to face something awful in our lives—and the chances are we will—what happens then? Will you freeze me *and* the baby out?'

He looked hurt. 'I'm older, now. Wiser. I hope.'

'You *hope*.' She knew she was being unfair, maybe even cruel, but this was too important to be swept under the carpet. 'But you can't be sure.'

'I talked to you after the lighthouse. And I told you things yesterday I'd never really talked about to anyone else.'

Which was a big thing for him, but it still wasn't enough to allay her fears. And the only way she could think of now was to tell him straight. 'What happens if it's something really awful—God forbid, if something happens to your mum or to Ruby? Or you get made redundant, or…' She blew out a breath. 'There are all sorts of things that could get in the way. How do you know you're not going to freeze me out again, next time things get tough?'

'Because I'll try harder, this time. I know

where I messed up. I won't repeat my mistakes.'

He might not intend to, but she could see the panic in his eyes. He might not be able to help himself. 'If it was just me to consider, I might take the risk. But, as you said, we have a baby to think of now.' She raked a hand through her hair. 'I say "baby". At this stage it's just a handful of cells.'

He went white. 'Are you suggesting…?'

'A termination? No.' She shook her head. 'That's not the answer for me. I'm keeping the baby. I know Mum and Dad will be there for me—your mum and Ruby will be there, too. I'll have support as a single mum.'

His eyes were very, very dark. 'Is that what you want? To bring the baby up on your own and have nothing to do with me?'

'No,' she said tiredly. 'Of course I don't want that. We'd make arrangements for access. I'd never keep the baby from you. Your family will be very much part of this baby's life.'

'My family, but not me.'

'You're three hours away, Brad. In London. It's not a workable situation for a relationship, living that far apart.' She blew out a breath. 'And that's something else we haven't discussed.' Where they'd live, if they tried to make a second go of their marriage. There was so very much to think about, and she wasn't sure she could do this. 'I don't expect you to leave London and come back here.'

'My career's in London.' He paused. 'But I could retrain. I could teach chemistry in secondary school. The education authority is crying out for science teachers.'

'You'd hate every second of it. You love the lab—you always have, and you always will. I could see you working with undergraduates, maybe, but only in a job where you got to do a big chunk of research as well. I won't ask you to give that up.'

His expression was very serious. 'And you love your job here. Not just the job, the place. And your family's here. I can't ask you to give that up.'

She shook her head in sheer frustration. 'I can't see any way to compromise, Brad. If we're to be together, one of us has to move and uproot everything.'

'So what's your solution?' he asked.

Not moving to London. Not being isolated with a small baby, hours away from her family and with Brad working ridiculous hours at the lab so she and their child would barely see him.

'I don't know.' She swallowed miserably. 'I

thought tonight we were going to talk about things. About what we want.'

'Then let's do that. What do you want, Abby?'

Him. And the baby. And her business. *Everything.*

Which was greedy.

She couldn't have it all.

And if she told him what she really wanted… He'd already offered to retrain as a school teacher and move back here, two things she knew he'd hate. How could she ask him to do that? It would only make him miserable, and in the end he'd grow to resent her and the baby. Their marriage would crumble again, only this time there'd be someone else hurt by the fallout.

She couldn't see any way out of it.

She was about to tell him so when his phone shrilled.

To her surprise, he ignored it.

'Brad, that might be important.'

'Then whoever it is will either leave a message or ring back,' he said.

His phone went again, and this time he glanced at the screen before rejecting the call.

'Who was it?' she asked.

'Sunetra.'

His number two at the lab. She frowned.

'Brad, it's eight o'clock at night. That's not a normal time to ring someone about work. So it must be important.'

'You're more important than work.'

That made her feel slightly better, but if she'd had a call about work at this time of the evening she'd know there was a problem and she'd want to act on it. 'Call her back,' she said.

He sighed, but did so; though Abigail couldn't tell from his side of the conversation if there was a problem or what Sunetra wanted from him.

When he ended the conversation, he looked at her. 'The reason it's late is because Sunetra was staying on to wait for some results in the lab. It seems we might have had a bit of a breakthrough and she wanted to let me know.'

'That's good, isn't it?'

'Yes.' But he didn't look as excited about it as she'd expected. 'I'm going to ring my boss and tell him I need to stay here for a bit longer.'

She shook her head. 'Brad, it sounds as if your team needs you there. You can't let them down. You have a responsibility to them— just as I have a responsibility to my team.'

'I know, but I don't want to let *you* down, Abby.'

He was clearly torn between his duty to

work and his duty to her. But he hadn't mentioned a word about his feelings towards her, just about his responsibilities. So she'd make this easy for him.

'We're at stalemate. And maybe we need some time apart to think.'

Time apart to think.

Brad had been here before. Five years ago. And that was where it had all unravelled. Time apart had turned into a divorce.

'No.'

She frowned. 'What do you mean, no?'

'No, we don't need time apart to think. We need time *together* to think.' He raked a hand through his hair. 'You're right—I do need to be in London. But I want to be here with you.'

'You can't be in two places at once. And you have responsibilities at work.'

'Last time you said we needed time apart to think, I let you go—and it was the worst decision I ever made,' he said. 'I'm not making that mistake again.'

'I'm not the one who's going, this time.'

'Fair point. And this isn't an open-ended thing. Because I'll be back tomorrow night. Whatever promises I have to make, whatever I have to do to make things work in the lab, I'll be back for you tomorrow. We'll both have had time to think about the baby and what we want. And we're going to talk, Abby. I'm going back to London now, but this isn't over. Not by a long way.'

He drove her back to her cottage. As he parked outside, he really wanted to kiss Abby and tell her he loved her and make a family with her, but he didn't want to put any pressure on her. He wanted her to be with him because she wanted to be with him, not because she thought she had a duty to the baby.

'I'll see you tomorrow,' he said.

She looked as if she didn't quite believe him, and that hurt. Yes, he'd let her down in the past—but they were both older and wiser. Faced with that same situation, he knew they'd both do things differently now.

'Have a safe journey,' she said. 'Text me when you get back.'

'It'll be late.'

'That's OK. Just text me.'

'OK.'

For a moment, he thought she was going to reach over and kiss him. And then he'd tell her that he loved her and never wanted to let her go again.

But she didn't.

She just looked bone-deep tired and miserable.

Which was pretty much how he felt, too, and he hated having to leave. Though he knew she was right. He had responsibilities and there were conversations he really needed to have at work. Because, even if Abby didn't want to be with him any more, she was having his baby. And he wanted to be there for her and their child. He didn't want to be the dad who turned up on the odd weekend and took the child to the playground and a fast-food place. He wanted to be part of their lives. Be there for every scan and antenatal class, the first day at nursery and the first day at school, all the nativity plays and sports days.

He waited until Abby was safely back inside the cottage before he drove back to London. And he thought about their situation all the way back.

She was right in that he didn't want to teach in a secondary school. He'd miss his work in the lab so much. But if it was a choice between doing a job he didn't love and being with the woman he loved, or doing the job he loved and being without Abby, then it would be an easy decision. He wanted to be with her and the job came second. He wanted a second chance with her and he wanted to see their child grow up. Most of all he wanted to make a proper family with Abby.

The way she saw it, either she had to give up her entire life and move to London to be with him, or he had to give everything up and move back to Norfolk.

But surely there had to be a middle way, where they could both get what they wanted?

He thought about it some more.

The previous summer, a headhunter had called him and offered him a job up in Manchester. He'd considered it seriously and had almost accepted, but in the end he'd talked to his boss and negotiated more responsibility in his job.

Maybe he could talk to the headhunter to see if anything was available nearer to Great Crowmell than London. Maybe Cambridge; it would still be two hours away from Great Crowmell, but that was better than three hours. More doable.

The next morning, he was in the lab early, but before he left the house he'd already bought flowers online to be delivered to Abby at breakfast time, along with the message *See you tonight. B.* Again, he'd been close to writing *I love you*, but he didn't want to pressure her. Just let her know that he wasn't going to let her down.

He'd also left a message with the headhunter he'd spoken to, outlining his availability and saying that he'd call at lunchtime to discuss the options.

He sorted out his team's questions, agreed the next steps for the project, and then went to speak to his boss.

'Good to have you back, Brad,' Dominic said.

This was where Brad knew he was supposed to say that it was good to be back. Which it was; and at the same time it wasn't.

'Can I be frank with you, Dominic?' he asked.

'Sure.'

'There isn't an easy way to say this, because I love my job here and I love working with my team—but I need to move out of London. I'm sorry, but I'm going to have to resign without seeing the project through to the end.'

'Move out of London?' Dominic frowned. 'Why? Is there a problem at home? Is there anything we can help with?'

Brad shook his head. 'It's all a bit up in the air at the moment, to be honest—it's for personal reasons.'

'OK.'

Dominic had been a great support. The least Brad could do was tell him the truth. 'I know you won't tell anyone before I'm ready to break the news.' Brad looked his boss straight in the eye. 'I just found out that I'm going to be a dad. And that's something I can't do from three hours away. It's not commutable, and I don't want to be a part-time dad.'

'No, of course not.' Dominic blinked. 'Well, this is a bit out of left field. I didn't even realise you were seeing someone, let alone that it was serious enough to start a family. I don't know what to say—um, congratulations?'

'I'm seeing my ex,' Brad said, 'and the baby wasn't planned. But I'm hoping we're going to be able to make things work, second time round.'

'As you're resigning, does that mean you have another job lined up?'

'Not yet,' Brad admitted. 'I might end up retraining. I was thinking of maybe teaching chemistry.'

'And you'd be happy doing that?'

'If it meant I could be with Abby and the baby, yes. But that's plan B,' Brad admitted. 'I'm keeping my options open.'

'If you want my opinion,' Dominic said, 'I think you'd hate teaching in a school because you'd miss the research side too much. And I also think you'd be a huge loss to the industry if you switched to teaching. I wish there was some way to keep you here, because I don't want to lose you.' He frowned. 'Would your partner consider moving to London?'

'That would mean moving a three-hour drive away from both our families. So if she moved here, that would mean she'll be pregnant and know nobody in the area—or, if she waited until the baby was born before she moved, she'd have a small baby and know nobody in the area. It's not fair to do that to her.'

'She'd make friends at antenatal classes, and at the baby groups.'

Abby would make friends easily, Brad knew. But that wasn't the issue. 'I don't want to make her uproot everything. And, to be honest, I know how much she loves it back in Norfolk. It's not just her home and her family, it's her family business as well.' Last time, Abby had put him first, uprooted herself and gone with him to Cambridge—and he'd let her down. This time, it was his turn to make the move. To put her first. 'So I need to go back to Norfolk.'

'Don't hand your notice in just yet,' Dominic said. 'Give me a few days. I know people in other labs. People I trained with. They're always looking for good people. One of them might have an opening.'

'I was going to sign on with an agency,

too,' Brad said. 'Talk to the people who head-hunted me last year.'

'Much as I'm going to hate losing you from the team, it looks as if you've got it all sorted out.' Dominic rolled his eyes. 'Not that I'd expect anything less from you. Your organisational skills put everyone else's to shame.'

'Obviously I'll work out my notice,' Brad said, 'but I have a lot of time in lieu owing.'

'I'm sure the HR team can work something out,' Dominic said. 'Thank you for being honest with me.' He sighed. 'I really wish you weren't going. But I understand. You must really, really love her.'

'I do,' Brad said. 'I was the one who messed it up, last time. And I'm going to be the one to fix it, this time.'

Who would be ringing her doorbell at this time of the morning? Abigail wondered.

Thankfully she'd always been a lark rather than an owl, so she was already up and dressed.

She answered the door to see a delivery man half hidden behind a huge bouquet of flowers.

'Ms Scott?'

'Yes.'

'These are for you. Could you sign for them, please?' The delivery man gave her the handset so she could sign on the screen, then handed her the flowers.

'Thank you,' she said, and took the flowers into the kitchen.

They were gorgeous, bright and summery, all yellows and blues.

But who would be sending her flowers—especially at this time of the morning, when it was well before normal delivery times? Someone had definitely pulled some strings or paid a massive premium to get them to her before she went to work.

Brad?

Her heart gave a little leap of excitement.

And then she thought about it. Were the flowers his way of saying sorry, he wasn't going to make it tonight?

Her hands shook slightly as she opened the envelope.

And the message left her none the wiser.

See you tonight. B.

Not even a kiss. Nothing emotional at all. She still didn't have a clue how he felt.

On the other hand, he'd got the flowers to her at a crazy time. And this didn't look like any old bouquet. He'd asked them to include little yellow pompom chrysanthemums with dark centres that looked like tiny sunflowers, flowers she'd admired in the stately home gardens with him earlier in the week. It was a detail she knew hadn't slipped past him. He'd chosen them deliberately because he knew she liked them.

And maybe he'd just sent them to let her know he wasn't going to let her down. This time. A statement that he'd be there tonight and then they'd talk properly.

A tear leaked down her cheek.

She so wanted this to work out. But, for that to happen, one of them was going to have to make a huge sacrifice—and the whole thing scared her stupid.

She rested one hand across her abdomen. 'Whatever happens, baby, you're going to be loved. I can guarantee that,' she said. But whether she and Brad would be living together and bringing their child up together— and where—she really didn't know.

She picked up her phone and texted him.

Thank you for the flowers. They're beautiful. Loved the pompoms. See you tonight.

And please, please let it work out.

* * *

The Friday night traffic was worse than usual, Brad thought.

He'd left London at six, hoping the worst of the rush hour would be over and he could get to Abby by nine—but there seemed to be roadworks and temporary traffic lights everywhere, holding him up at every stage.

He called her at seven, but her mobile phone went through to voice mail; clearly she was either busy or she hadn't heard the phone ring. 'I'm on my way,' he said, 'but the traffic's terrible. I'll be with you as soon as I can.'

She didn't call him back, so either she hadn't picked up the message or she didn't want to talk to him. He really hoped it was the former. Sure, he could go and stay with his mother, or find a room in a hotel somewhere, and then sit on her doorstep the next morning until she emerged for her usual run, but he just wanted to be with Abby.

He was thoroughly fed up with sitting in a queue of traffic, but at least all the delays gave him a chance to practise what he wanted to say to Abby. He just hoped that she'd actually listen to him.

A phone call with news from Dominic, half an hour later, cheered him up slightly.

Though it was half-past nine before he

reached Great Crowmell, and it took him another ten minutes to find a parking space because the car park was much busier than he'd expected. But finally he knocked on Abigail's door.

She looked as if she hadn't slept properly the previous night, and there were dark smudges under her eyes.

'Sorry—I'm really late. Maybe it would be better to do this tomorrow,' he said.

'No, come in,' she said. 'Have you eaten?'

'Yes,' he lied. He didn't want food—he wanted Abby. And he didn't want to give her an excuse for distraction.

'At least let me make you a cup of coffee.'

'Not if the smell makes you feel queasy.'

'It's fine.' She bustled around the kitchen. 'Your flowers were lovely.'

'I got your message.' He smiled. 'I'm glad you noticed I picked the flowers deliberately.' The day they'd talked about going to Monet's garden together in the spring.

'How did you get someone to deliver so early?' she asked.

'The Internet can be a wonderful thing,' he said.

And then he couldn't stand it any more. 'Abby.'

'What?'

He took the tin of coffee from her and put it on the worktop, then drew her into his arms. 'I missed you.'

'You were only gone a day.'

That bright, breezy tone meant she was trying to hide her feelings. And it gave him hope. 'I still missed you.' He dragged in a breath. 'Forget the coffee. I need to tell you something.'

She went very still. 'Oh?'

Did she really think he was going to let her down again? He pulled back slightly, keeping his arms loosely round her but making sure she could see his eyes. Making sure she had no cause to doubt his sincerity. 'Last night, I tried not to put any pressure on you. But I'm done with trying to be noble. I need you to know the truth. Abigail Scott, you're the love of my life—you always have been, you always will be, and I want to be with you.'

She looked as if she was about to say something, and he gave the tiniest shake of his head. 'Hear me out, because I've been practising this all the way from London and I want to get it right. Five years ago, I was very, very stupid. I thought I was doing the right thing in letting you go in order to find the happiness you deserve with someone else. But it's the worst thing I ever did and I've regretted it every single day since. I bury myself in work so I don't have time to realise how empty my life is without you.

'But I want you back, Abby. I want you and I want our baby. I want the life we should've had together if I hadn't gone into meltdown when Dad died. And I don't want to be a part-time. Actually, I'm scared as hell I'll make as much of a mess of being a dad as I have of being a son, a brother and a husband, but I'm going to do whatever it takes to make this work. I want to be a full-time family, with you. I know you don't want to live in London because it's too far away from our family, so I'm moving back to Norfolk.'

She looked utterly shocked. 'But—' she began.

'Hear me out, Abby,' he said again. 'Yes, I love my job, but I love you more. If it's a choice between you, then you'll always win. I'm coming home to you.'

'But I don't want to give you an ultimatum, Brad. I don't want you to give up the job you love.'

'I don't have to,' he said. 'I didn't tell you, but last year I was headhunted to work for a company in Manchester. I turned it down because my boss gave me more responsibilities and I wanted to see my current project through, but I got in touch with the headhunters today to see if they had anything else available.'

'Did they?' She looked hopeful.

'No,' he said, 'but my boss trained with someone who runs a lab in Norwich, and he's put in a good word for me. It's not absolutely definite, and there are no guarantees I'll get the job, but they're ringing me on Monday to arrange an interview. It'll be a mix of lab work and teaching postgraduate students, which suits me fine. Plus my hours will be reasonable and it'll be only a forty-minute commute from here—that's less time than it takes me to get to my lab now. Even if they don't offer me the job, then I can find something. The main thing is I'll be here with you.' He took a deep breath. 'The first time I asked you this question, I pretty much knew the answer before I asked.' The second time, she'd said no. Would this be third time lucky? 'This time, I don't. It scares the hell out of me that you'll say the words I don't want to hear, but even if you do I'll be here for you and the baby. That's not going to change.' He swallowed hard, then dropped to one knee in front of her. 'I love you, Abby. I always will. Will you marry me and make a family with me and our baby?'

* * *

He loved her.

Loved her enough to put her before the job she thought was his life.

And he was telling her that she could have it all. She didn't have to wrench herself away from their family, she didn't have to give up her job to follow him—this time, he was making the changes. He'd found a compromise that would work for both of them. And he wanted to marry her again.

All she had to do was say yes.

'You shouldn't have to do all the compromising,' she said.

'You did all the compromising last time,' he said. 'So I think it's my turn.'

'Not necessarily,' she said. 'Maybe I could open a branch of Scott's in Norwich and run all the admin from there. Then you wouldn't have such a long commute.'

He coughed. 'Abby, that was a yes or no question. And you're killing me, making me wait for the answer. I'm not promising you perfection, because I'm only human. But I'll try my hardest not to let you down again. To be a much better husband than I was before and a good dad. I love you. Nobody else has ever come close to making me feel the way I feel about you.' He looked up at her, his eyes dark and beseeching. 'Will you marry me again? Make a family with me and our baby?'

She took his hand and drew him to his feet. 'I love you, too. Always have and always will. Yes, I'll marry you.'

He wrapped his arms round her and kissed her lingeringly. 'I was so scared you'd say no.'

'I never have been able to resist you, Brad. But it took me a long while to pick myself up again when you filed for divorce.'

'It was the worst mistake of my life,' he said. 'No more hair shirts and no more white chargers.'

'Agreed.' She paused. 'Though, this time round, I think we owe our family the party we deprived them of last time.'

'Absolutely.'

'And your sister gets to be my bridesmaid.' She smiled. 'And we pour a glass of champagne on your dad's grave so Jim gets to share it, too.'

'I'd like that.' He kissed her. 'All that time we wasted… We've got some making up to do.'

She grinned as he scooped her up into his arms and carried her out of the kitchen. 'I thought you'd never ask…'

EPILOGUE

A year later

'OK. YOU'RE DONE,' Gina, the hairdresser, said with a smile.

Abby looked at her reflection. 'I can barely believe this is me.'

'Wait until you've got the dress and shoes on,' Ruby said.

'Mummy looks amazing, doesn't she, Jessie?' Annie said, cuddling her granddaughter.

The baby gurgled, as if to agree, and everyone smiled.

Ruby helped Abby into her dress, straightened her veil and then stood back. 'Wow. You look amazing.'

Abby's dress was cream, with a full-length tulle skirt, and a bodice of raw silk with a spray of roses across it.

'So do you,' Abby said. Ruby's dress was similar to Abby's, but in duck-egg blue.

Ruby hugged her. 'I'm so thrilled to be get-

ting my sister back. Not that I ever didn't see
you as my sister. And I still can't believe you
got back together with Brad at my wedding.'

'Contagious things, weddings,' Abby said
with a grin, and hugged her back.

There was a knock on the door. 'Am I allowed in?' Stuart asked.

'Sure. It's just the bridegroom who's not
allowed,' Ruby said.

Stuart came in with a large box. 'Flowers.'

Both Abby and Ruby had simple bouquets
of cream roses and there was also a single red
rose from Brad.

I love you and I can't wait to marry you.

Abby blinked away the tears. She couldn't
wait to marry him, too.

'You look beautiful, love,' Stuart said.
'Let's go downstairs and have a glass of
champagne while we're waiting for the cars.
And I need a cuddle from this young lady
here.' He scooped Jessica from his wife's
arms and blew a raspberry at the baby, who
chuckled and waved her hands in glee.

Once the cars had arrived and Annie, Jessica
and Ruby had left, Stuart looked at his daughter. 'You and Brad seem settled,' he said quietly, 'but I need to know you're sure about this.'

'Absolutely sure,' Abby said. 'This is the wedding we should have had, the first time round—and this time it's for keeps.'

The first part of their wedding was a very small register office do, with just their immediate family attending; and then Brad kissed Abby. 'I love you,' he said. 'And this time our marriage is for keeps.'

'For keeps,' she agreed.

And then they headed to the church for the blessing, where the rest of their family and friends were waiting.

Brad waited at the top of the aisle. He turned round as the organist began to play the traditional 'Wedding March', to see Abby walking towards him. She was even more beautiful now than she'd been ten years ago when they had first married; and as she walked towards him he felt as if his whole body was bubbling with sheer happiness.

Although the blessing didn't involve an exchange of rings or giving away of the bride, they'd discussed the service with the vicar to make it feel as much like a wedding as possible, with Stuart and Rosie reading Shakespeare and Elizabeth Barrett Browning respectively, hymns, flowers and the church bell pealing as they walked back down the aisle after the service.

Everyone threw the bird-friendly confetti at them, and then while the photographer was organising some of the group shots they went to James's grave and poured a glass of champagne next to his headstone.

'I know you're here with us today in spirit, Jim,' Abby said. 'And I promise you I'll love your son for ever.'

'Sorry we eloped, the first time round,' Brad said. 'We're doing it right, this time. Sharing with our family and friends, the way we should've done last time.'

After the photographs had finished, they headed for the hotel—the one where they'd gone to the prom together and kissed for the very first time, because they'd both agreed that was the right place to hold their wedding breakfast.

And Brad felt happier than he'd ever thought possible as he sat at the table with his four-month-old daughter asleep on his lap, the love of his life next to him, and their family and friends surrounding them.

This time, they were doing it right.

Stuart kicked off the speeches after the meal, as the father of the bride. 'Welcome, everyone,' he said. 'I'm pleased to say that this time Abigail and Bradley didn't run off to Gretna Green—but I guess that's harder to do when you have a baby.' Everyone laughed. 'I'm going to keep this short, and say I'm delighted to welcome Brad back into the family, where he's always belonged,' Stuart said. 'Please raise your glasses to the bride and groom, Abby and Brad.'

'Abby and Brad,' everyone chorused.

Brad couldn't quite bear to wake Jessica by transferring her to his wife's arms, so he stood up and gave his speech with his daughter in his arms. 'I'd like to thank everyone for coming, and as Stuart said this time we didn't run off to Gretna Green. Actually, it wasn't so much because of Jessica, because she's happy to go anywhere, but we didn't think you'd forgive us for depriving you of a party for the second time.'

There were claps and hoots and cheers.

'Ten years on, we're both older and wiser—at least, I think we are,' Brad continued. 'I would like to thank Stuart, Annie, Mum and George for all their help over the wedding arrangements and for being wonderful grandparents; and I'd like to thank my twin Ruby for being the best bridesmaid ever. And I'd like you all to raise a glass to my gorgeous bride, Mrs Abby Powell—I'm so proud of her. For most people, moving house or having a baby or opening a new branch of the family business in a different town would be quite enough to do in a year. Not for my new wife, because she's done all three—and she was named local businesswoman of the year, last week. She's brilliant. And I'm very lucky she agreed to marry me again.' He lifted his glass. 'To Abby.'

'To Abby,' everyone echoed.

Colin stood up next. 'I'm absolutely thrilled that my brother-in-law chose me as best man. I knew he actually wanted his sister as his best woman, but his bride called first dibs on her, so he was pretty much stuck with me. So I'm going to keep it short and sweet—please raise your glasses to the bride and groom, Abby and Brad.'

And then Abby stood up. 'I'd like to thank you all for coming today. This is the wedding we probably should have given you last time, and I think it's fitting that we're celebrating here because this is the place where Brad and I first danced together at the school prom—he kissed me for the very first time in the rose garden here. I'd like to thank my parents for being brilliantly supportive about me moving some of the family business to Norwich, my parents again and Rosie and George for being wonderful grandparents and excellent babysitters, and Ruby—well, she never actually stopped being my sister as far as I was concerned, but it's nice for it to be official again. To Jessica, for being the sweetest-tempered baby in the world; to Jim, who I'm very sure is here with us in spirit; and most of all to Brad, the love of my life, for finding a compromise so we both won.' She smiled. 'Now we're done with all the talking bits—let's get this party started!'

Jessica was scooped up by Rosie. 'Go and have the first dance,' she said, shooing Brad and Abby onto the dance floor.

They walked into the centre, and the band started to play the song that Brad had danced to with Abby for the very first time, at the school prom: 'Make You Feel My Love.'

'We did it right, this time,' he said softly as they began to dance. 'Celebrating with all our family and friends—including our little girl.'

'Three magpies,' she said.

He smiled. 'The old superstition turned out to be right. And I'm the luckiest man on earth. Thank you for giving me a second chance.'

'This time,' she said, 'it's for keeps. You and me. Always.'

'Always,' he said, and kissed her.

* * * * *

If you enjoyed this story,
check out these other great reads
from Kate Hardy

Christmas Bride for the Boss
The Runaway Bride and the Billionaire
His Shy Cinderella
Her Festive Doorstep Baby

All available now!